## Early Praise for
## *Tales by Moons-light:*
## *Stories from before the Great Melt*

Mom's Choice Gold Award winner and Blue Ink Review Notable Book!

"Ballard's fantastical collection of stories blends elements of fairy tale, fable, and sci-fi for a strikingly imaginative feat of storytelling. The characters seen throughout these tightly woven, seamless stories, are whimsical and distinctive, peculiar and performative. Each individual plays perfectly into the dynamic and wonderfully inventive universe Ballard creates for them."

—Judge's critique, BookLife Prize

"Ballard's writing is stellar. Her tales unfold seamlessly with inventive, imaginative plots and a creative cast of characters, both human and animal."

— BlueInk Review

"In each story, children face a diverse set of challenges that spark them to find their inner power, whether it be courage, a voice, problem-solving abilities, or the rescue of another. Each story provides a very different scenario that is as compellingly written as the last."

—Midwest Book Reviews

"The stories distinguish themselves in their considerable definition and physical details, though their themes and character types evoke traditional fairy tales: a son's deformity results in inner strength; children's unlucky fortunes... them together; a greedy father's bar... to a husband she cannot love. Some ...

D1430849

to outwit fate and unsavory adults to achieve their goals; elsewhere, characters appealing to younger readers sleep in down-filled "ducky sacks." Charming illustrations rendered in pen, ink, and wash suggest the diversity, rich colors, and beauty of Urth, its people, and its animals... Representing a mix of ages, the otherworldly fairy tales collected in *Tales by Moons-light* are imaginative and charming."

—Susan Waggoner, Foreword Reviews

"Ballard is truly a pioneer of children's literature with this book. When science fiction meets fantasy, a whole new genre is born. She takes the reader on a journey that leaves them transported in realms where the imagination can roam freely. Time is skewed where there are two moons and characters roam unfamiliar terrain. Yet, her fables have a fairy-tale quality that taps into the timeless magic of once upon a time. Her ability to blend science with fantasy is the future of children's literature. I highly recommend this book!"

—Alanna Wright
*Founder, Academic Goals tutoring company*

"I read *Tales by Moons-light: Stories from before the Great Melt* to my seven-year-old daughter, and it sparked her curiosity and imagination more than any other book we've enjoyed together. After reading the first story, *The Moons-lings*, we starting tracking the moon from night to night. We even recreated the orbits of Urth's two moons on a white board, using movable magnets for Urth, Lunera, and Ru! This book is a fantastic teaching tool, and I recommend it to parents and teachers who want to introduce scientific concepts to children through terrific storytelling."

—A. Green, Las Vegas, NV

"If you only read one story in this amazing book, make it The Poison Well. This fable teaches children the importance of protecting and preserving the ecosystem in which they live, and on which their lives depend. This is such an important message, and we need our kids to embrace it. I'll be using this story in my third-grade classroom, and am already spreading the word to my colleagues!"

—B. Garcia, Los Angeles, CA

"I really liked all the stories, but my favorite was The Six Woes of Werd. I loved the ways that new woes replaced old ones, and the idea that woes plague only the living."

—Ava, age 11, Sacramento, CA.

"Once I started reading this book, I couldn't put it down! The stories are fun, exciting, interesting, and just the right length to read before bed. There are seven tales in all, and I was planning to spread them out across a week, but I ended up reading the book from beginning to end, in one sitting! They all have fun twists and turns, but I liked The Rule of E the best. The main character outwitted her evil grandfather, and a pompous prince, in such a clever way!"

—Eleanor, age 13, Grade 8

"These tales spin magic and science together. It is the job of the reader to unscramble the clues! I enjoyed this book because it is easy to read, entertaining, and unique. I would recommend this book to other young readers who enjoy captivating tales that take you to another world!"

—Shreya, age 10, City Book Reviews

# Tales

*by* **Moons-light**

OTHER BOOKS IN THE
# Tales by Moons-light Series

---

*Frankie and the Gift of Fantasy*

*Elvia and the Gift of Passion*

# Tales by Moons-light

RUTHY BALLARD

WHIPSMART
BOOKS

STORIES FROM
BEFORE THE
Great Melt

Names: Ballard, Ruthy, author.
Title: Tales by moons-light : [stories from before the Great Melt]
   / Ruthy Ballard.
Description: Sacramento, California : WhipSmart Books, [2021]
   | Series: Tales by moons-light series ; [2] | Interest age level:
   009-012. | Summary: Presents seven tales from a distant,
   two-mooned planet called Urth.
Identifiers: ISBN 9780997853247 (paperback) | ISBN
   9780997853254 (Kindle) | ISBN 9780997853261 (ePub)
Subjects: LCSH: Planets--Juvenile fiction. | Wizards--Juvenile
   fiction. | Fortune-tellers--Juvenile fiction. | Survival--Juvenile
   fiction. | Kidnapping--Juvenile fiction. | CYAC: Planets--Fic-
   tion. | Wizards--Fiction. | Fortune-tellers--Fiction. | Surviv-
   al--Fiction. | Kidnapping--Fiction. | LCGFT: Science fiction. |
   Fantasy fiction. | Short stories.
Classification: LCC PZ7.1.B35 Ta 2021 (print) | LCC PZ7.1.B35
   (ebook) | DDC [Fic]--dc23


WhipSmart Books

Sacramento, California
www.whipsmartbooks.com

To Irene, who has the gift of *Caring for Others*

"Science demystifies the world.

Fables make sense of it."

—JOHN DOBSON
*Astronomer, Philosopher, Renegade, and Pied Piper*

# Contents

# Acknowledgments

Writing this book was largely a solo enterprise, and, in the early days of creative flurry, I spent many magical hours alone in the cozy "look out" above my art studio, pounding happily away on my laptop. Taking the book to publication, however, was another story; it took a crew, and I owe a profound debt of gratitude to those who helped me navigate those less-familiar waters.

The WhipSmart Books' publishing team includes seasoned professionals who worked together, in coordinated fashion, to steer the project true north. Early on, publishing navigator Janica Smith and marketer Gail Kearns took the helm. Later, professional editors, including the incomparable Jenny Bowman, made timely adjustments, while the book designers, Alan Hebel and Ian Koviak, harnessed their creative talents to raise the sail, full speed to the wind.

My family and friends contributed, too, by reading innumerable drafts, offering treasured insights, and encouraging me to "keep on keeping on" during the inevitable doldrums. Of these angels, my husband Ernie Hills was the most belabored, working both above and below decks for the duration of the voyage, as my First Mate, Cook, and Watch Leader. With his dual gifts of *Taking Care of Others* and *Swinging to Latin Jazz*, he spent countless evenings whipping up delicious dinners (headphones on and fingers snapping), while ensuring that our zoo of cats and dogs never missed a meal, either.

I'm also grateful to the early influencers who shaped my world view. As a child, I marinated in the delightful works of C.S. Lewis, Dr. Seuss, Norton Juster, Betty MacDonald, Caroline Keene, and Ira and Mae Freeman, among many others. I can still remember the thrill of reading *You Will Go to the Moon*, a book that kindled my interest in the cosmos. In my late teens and early twenties, John Dobson, of Sidewalk Astronomers fame, and Sacramento State astronomy professor Homer Ibser, fueled the flames. At 17, I built my first telescope, and over the ensuing years, I ventured to the National Parks in the summers, where I shared views of the moon, the planets, and distant galaxies with the general public, under spectacularly dark skies. I learned the basics of celestial navigation and the true nature of who I was: a child of an exploded star that, long ago, fused simple gasses into the more complex elements of carbon, oxygen, nitrogen, and phosphorous: the building blocks of life.

Lastly, the children in the WhipSmart Books' Early Reader Program inspired me with their generosity and precocious wisdom. Like the characters in the final chapter of the book, "True Tale at the Equator," they reviewed the manuscript from different perspectives, and helped me hone it for a wide audience, while honoring the stories' plots and messages. These young people, who are newly afloat on wonderous journeys of their own, are listed below, and I wish them brisk winds and grand adventures along the way. Thank you!

Barron, Age 8, Falls Church, VA

Ava, age 11, Sacramento, CA

Maria Grace, age 7, Las Vegas, NV

Arsenio, age 10, Los Angeles, CA

Nate, age 11, Reno, NV

Eleanor, age 13, Rancho Cordova, CA

Anna, age 11, Rancho Cordova, CA

Michael, age 10, San Jose, CA

Clarice, age 12, Houston, TX

Melody Ann, age 13, Jacksonville, FL

Mateo, age 11, Portland, OR

Madison, age 10, Chicago, IL

Trevor, age 11, Spokane, WA

Allison, age 13, Houston, TX

Sam, age 10, Chico, CA

Devon, age 11, Colorado Springs, CO

Madeline, age 10, Arlington, VA

Anthem, age 9, Burlington, VT

Lourdes Rose, age 13, Reno, NV

# Prologue

At exactly 14:00 hours Universal Mean Time on February 5, 1961, twelve-year-old Blessing Okoro shot through a space-time tunnel that links a distant planet called Urth with Earth, arriving home precisely four months, three days, two hours, and eight minutes after she'd mysteriously disappeared.

Like children everywhere, Blessing had a special gift, and hers was the delightful one of *Breaking Rules*. Thus, despite the fact that she'd been warned not to, she grabbed *Tales by Moons-light: Stories from Before the Great Melt* and stole it, anyway. Then she squirreled it away under her bed, enclosing a brief note summarizing her adventure, and promptly forgot about her journey. As happens to most children who return from Urth, a strange amnesia settled over her, so she didn't blink an eye when her mother donated the precious

1

cargo to the local library a few weeks later.

It was only by sheer luck that I stumbled on it there. I'd been to Urth, too, but, unlike Blessing, I remembered my trip and knew the book for what it was: a collection of stories that took place hundreds to thousands of years ago before a catastrophe—the Great Melt—reduced Urth's land surface to islands. Told and retold, Urth people passed the stories down through the generations, weaving fact with fiction until it was difficult to untwist the two. In some of the tales, animals with mixed-up names talk to the people they love, or fly through outer space, where there's no air to keep them aloft. Yet, the *"moons-science"* is real (Urth has two moons, Lunera and Ru), and, as a reader, you may enjoy unraveling fact from fantasy, especially if you like solving puzzles.

Astonished to find the precious book, I checked it out with no intention of returning it. Instead, I held onto it, and, as I grew older, I selected a handful of my favorite stories to edit for Earth children. I added facts as I remembered them, and illustrations as I remembered them, too, and then a glossary and pronunciation guide.

The special edition for Earth children you're now reading is the result of that effort, and, after a preview version of the book was released, Blessing, all grown up, brought her grandson to a book signing. She stood in line with a wistful look, as if unsure why she'd come, and I noticed that she clung to her grandson's hand very tightly, as if he might be whisked away from her at any moment.

When it was Blessing's turn, I wanted to thank her for what she'd done, and tell her my secret: why I remembered my own amazing journey across the galaxy while she did not. But there was no point. She didn't remember Urth and never would. Instead, I buried my secret in the stories themselves, hoping that a clever reader with the gift of *Smarts* would figure it out.

# 1

# The Moons-lings

*In which a brilliant girl outwits a sorceress.*

It was a dark and moons-less night, many centuries ago, before the Great Melt, when a girl named Margie, and her younger brother Hal, were snatched from their "ducky sacks" by an evil sorceress who called herself Auntie.

"Your parents don't want you anymore," the sorceress told them. Then she forced them to drink some asleep tea to make her mission easier, and whisked them off to her castle far away.

This was not the first time the sorceress had stolen children. She had fifteen under her control already. She kept them as slaves, forcing them to clean her huge castle from dawn to dusk and cook her meals. Yet, no matter how hard they worked, there was always more for them to do. The castle had a hundred rooms, each

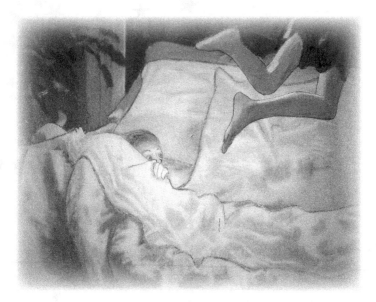

*Margie and Hal were snatched from their ducky sacks...*

with an enormous statue of Auntie in the middle and an
intimidating wall of stained-glass windows.

The children were miserable, but they didn't dare com-
plain. The sorceress made terrible threats that kept them
quiet and obedient.

The morning after their abduction, the horrible
woman beckoned Margie and Hal to her. It was time to
terrorize them.

"I control the sun," she claimed, her black eyes flash-
ing. "I've made the days longer, and the nights longer, too.
And I rule Urth's two moons. I have vanquished Lunera
from the skies and brought Ru under my strict com-
mand. I can draw Ru close to me whenever I like, which
is a dreadful sight. So you must do what I say, like all the

others, and never question my authority."

Hal was younger than Margie, and when the sorceress told these lies, he believed them. But Margie was older and unusually smart. She didn't fall under Auntie's spell so easily.

"No one can control the sun and the moons," she told herself, "and our parents didn't abandon us. Something strange is happening, but I will figure it out. Meanwhile, I must protect Hal from this woman's wickedness."

The sorceress didn't want her captured children to talk to one another. She was fearful they would launch a rebellion. So she assigned Margie and Hal the task of scrubbing the flagstone floor in the attic room at the top of the castle. An Urth bird called a "nerva" lived up there, high in the rafters, and pooped on the floor at regular intervals. So once Margie and Hal had finished cleaning, the floor was dirty again, and they had to start all over.

Just as the sorceress had predicted, the first day lasted a very long time, followed by a night that went on and on for many Urth days. And she called the mighty moon Ru to her, until it was weirdly huge in the sky, getting bigger and bigger as the long night dragged on, until it was so close that the captured children hid in every dark corner and closet, terrified it would gobble them up whole.

Margie shuttled Hal into a large wardrobe in the attic room where they worked, for he was too petrified to speak. She was frightened, too, and didn't dare

*The sorceress called the mighty moon Ru to her...*

look up to where Ru glared down at them through the high windows.

It was during this terrible time that the nerva introduced itself, flying down to Margie's shoulder.

Margie had never seen such a spectacular nerva. It was so old that its head feathers had turned white. Its eyes were ruby red, and its silver beak glowed in Ru's orange light.

"Don't be scared," the nerva squawked, looking straight into Margie's eyes, with fierce intelligence. "We can escape from this castle if you solve three riddles."

"Oh, nerva," Margie cried, suddenly full of hope. "My teachers say I'm a smart girl. I will try to solve the

riddles. Hal and I want to go
home, where we belong."

The nerva cocked its head
to one side, sizing her up.

"I have been imprisoned in
this castle since I was a fledg-
ling. I've been here many years
and am eager to see Urth, where
I was born. But I can only fly
away if one of Auntie's children solves the riddles."

*"Don't be scared," the
nerva squawked...*

"Are they difficult?"

"The good news is that when you solve one riddle,
you solve them all. The bad news is that fifteen children
before you have tried and failed. But I sense that *you*
might have a brain that's up to the task. Perhaps you can
solve the riddles. Then we can escape."

Margie leapt at the chance. "Tell me the first riddle.
I am eager to get started," she pleaded.

"Then here it is," the nerva replied. "Open wide your
ears. You must hear every word."

Margie leaned in, and the nerva said:

> *Why are the days and nights so long?*
> *For Auntie does not control the sun.*

Then it flew back up into the rafters.

Margie frowned. It was a difficult problem. But
she knew that the nerva was telling the truth. The sun
didn't bend to Auntie's will. That's not the way the world

worked. There had to be another explanation.

Margie thought long and hard about the riddle and grew half an inch before she had an idea.

"I know why the days and nights are so long," she cried one morning, at the beginning of another lengthy day. "Come down from the rafters and hear what I have to say, oh nerva. I've solved the first riddle!"

The nerva appeared on her shoulder once more.

"We're at the North Pole," Margie said excitedly. "In school, we studied the explorers who ventured there. At the North Pole, the days are very long—nearly half a year. Likewise, the nights are half a year, too. That solves the riddle. Now may Hal and I go home?"

The nerva flashed its red eyes and shook its head in disappointment.

"It is a fine idea," it replied. "You are, indeed, a bright girl. But the days and nights here aren't nearly as long as half a year, are they?"

Margie had to admit that this was true.

"Besides," the nerva continued, "your explanation does not solve the second riddle."

"Oh, nerva," Margie pleaded, "then tell me the second riddle. I am eager to get started."

"Then here it is," the nerva replied. "Open wide your ears. You must hear every word."

*Why has Lunera disappeared from the skies?*
*For Auntie does not control Lunera.*

Margie pondered the second riddle as she and Hal scrubbed the flagstone floors and, at Auntie's orders, began cleaning the statue in the center of the room.

"Not a trace of dirt must remain, my children, or I will unleash my full powers and order the sun to burn you to a crisp."

As she slaved away, Margie contemplated everything she knew about Lunera, Urth's brightest and closest moon. It was locked in tidal orbit, always presenting its "front side" to the Urth. No one knew what was on the "back side," always out of view.

"I can't understand it," Margie told Hal as they worked. "It will be difficult to find an answer that solves the two riddles, but I won't give up, for I want us to get home, where we belong."

*"I can't understand it," Margie said...*

More time passed, and Margie grew another half inch before she had a new idea.

"I know the answer," she cried one evening, at the beginning of another drawn-out night. "Come down from the rafter, nerva, and hear what I have to say. I've solved *both* riddles."

The nerva appeared on her shoulder once more, listening intently.

"We *are* at the North Pole," Margie said, "but it's winter. I learned in school that Lunera follows the same path as the sun as it moves through the background stars, or nearly so. When you're at the North Pole in the winter, Lunera, like the sun, never rises or sets. It can't be seen. That's why the days and nights are so long and Lunera has disappeared from view."

The nerva shook its head sadly. "No, no, no," it replied. "If we were at the North Pole, and it was winter, the sun would never rise or set like it does here. What's more, Lunera would be visible at least some of the time. Indeed, it would be visible half the month, from first

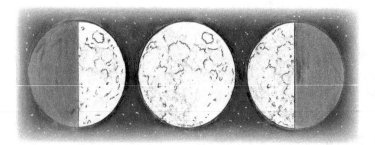

*The moon would be visible from first quarter to third...*

quarter to third, shining brightly on the ice. You must try harder, for all of our sakes."

Margie sighed. Moons-studies was a difficult subject, and so confusing that most children in her class had not yet passed the course, including herself.

"But I mustn't lose faith in my abilities," she thought determinedly. "I just need to think this through, one step at a time."

She persevered.

"Oh, nerva," she pleaded, "tell me the third riddle. I need another clue, so I can end this game."

"Then here it is," the nerva said. "Open wide your ears. You must hear every word."

*Why does Ru get so huge in the sky?*
*For Auntie does not control Ru.*

Margie was stumped, but she didn't give up, even as the sorceress gave them another terrible chore, this one even more challenging than the others.

"Clean the high windows until they shine," she demanded. "If I find a trace of dirt, even in the crevices, I will banish you to the depths of airless space, where you'll suffocate."

Margie and Hal dragged a large ladder into the room so they could begin their daunting task. And all the while, Margie pondered the third riddle, wondering if she'd ever be able to find the truth that would collapse all three riddles into one.

*"Clean the high windows," Auntie demanded...*

A long time passed, and Margie grew another half an inch while she and Hal worked on the windows.

"You will clean the rafters next," the sorceress demanded, not stopping to praise them one whit for the work they'd already done so well. "You will need a second ladder, now. I want the job done quickly."

She rattled off another threat and then disappeared down the stairs, leaving them alone, again, with a task that seemed impossible.

As they climbed to the top of their respective ladders to begin their toil, Margie scanned her memory for everything she knew about Ru, Urth's dimmer moon. It was farther away than Lunera, and orange in hue. But it never got bigger and smaller in the skies back home, not the way it did here. Whatever its phase, from full to new, it never changed its diameter, only its *shape*, from round to a skinny crescent.

*Whatever its phase, from full to new, it never changed its diameter, only its shape...*

More days and nights crawled past, and Margie grew
yet again. They were done with the rafters now, and she
was tired out, defeated by the hard work and the three
riddles. She was ready to give up as she climbed down
the ladder one last time.

When she got to the flagstone floor, Margie glanced
over at Hal, who had descended from *his* ladder, too.
He'd been laboring on a different section of the rafters,
on the opposite side of the statue of Auntie. And, directly
behind him, from Margie's perspective, was the wall of
windows, bright with sunlight.

Margie paused, transfixed, and a thrill shot through
her. She'd suddenly had an idea so astonishing that her
heart beat like a hammer and her hands trembled.

Seeing the change in his sister, Hal rushed over, but
Margie ordered him to go back to his ladder.

"I have it!" she cried! "Oh, Hal, I understand everything. All three riddles make sense."

Hal eyed her curiously. She'd been wrong twice
before, but he could see from the sparkle in her eyes
that this time might be different.

She exclaimed, "Imagine that the wall of windows is
the sun and the statue of Auntie is Urth itself."

Hal was only a little boy, but he had the gift of *Painting
Pictures in His Mind*. He quickly and easily transformed
the wall of windows into Urth's sun and the statue of
Auntie into planet Urth, using his colorful imagination.

Margie was aware of her brother's skill and knew he

was following along, so she continued.

"Now imagine that *I* am Lunera, and *you* are Ru, on opposite sides of Urth."

Hal did so, his sister morphing into a bright white moon, while he himself became an orange one.

"Okay," Margie continued. "Now you stay put, and I will circle the statue of Auntie, remembering that Lunera is locked in tidal orbit, always presenting its 'front side' to Urth, never its 'back side.'"

Hal watched as Margie traced her path, following the month-long cycle of Lunera. Because Lunera was closer to the Urth than Ru, Margie (Lunera) passed between Hal (Ru) and the statue of Auntie (Urth) as she went. At one point, she was directly between Hal and the statue, so close that he could reach out and touch her (which he did). Then she moved past him and retreated, circling back to her original position.

When the cycle was complete, Margie smiled at him triumphantly.

"It's just as I suspected," she cried. "I saw the wall of windows—the sun—exactly half the time. One long day and one long night, each lasting half a Lunera month, about twelve days each. We're on Lunera, you and I. That's why the days and nights are so long—but not so long as half a year—and why we never see Lunera in the sky. It's beneath our feet!"

Hal was amazed. Could it be true? Were they standing on a moon?

"But what about the *third* riddle?" he asked after his astonishment had eased. "The one about Ru?"

"I can explain that, too," she assured him, her excitement at a fever pitch. "As I circled the statue, I passed close to you, didn't I, when we were both on the *same* side of it? But now that we're on *opposite* sides, I am far away. Do you understand?"

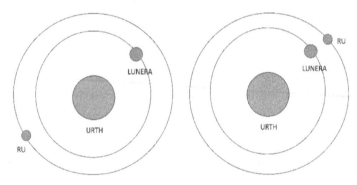

*Depending on where they are in their orbits,*
*Urth's moons can be close together or far apart...*

Hal nodded, and his eyes widened, as an "aha!" moment of understanding illuminated his mind.

"I see it all at last!" Margie cried, racing over to Hal and lifting him into her arms. "Auntie doesn't have the power to draw Ru close to us whenever she likes. Ru comes, anyway, on a regular schedule, following the laws of nature."

Hal replied, "Auntie lied. She's been lying the whole time!"

Margie planted a kiss on Hal's cheek and cried out

with glee, "Come down from the rafters, nerva, and hear what I have to say. I've solved all three riddles!"

The nerva, who'd been listening in, was ecstatic that Margie had finally figured things out. Thrilled, it cascaded down from the rafters, its wings beating the air. But it didn't land on her shoulder this time. Instead, it landed at her feet and grew bigger and bigger and bigger, until it was the size of a "sehor," an Urth mammal much like a horse.

"You are a *brilliant* girl!" the nerva boomed, its voice much deeper now that it was so huge. "You've broken Auntie's spell! But I have one more question, one that's puzzled me for years. If we're on Lunera, why don't we see Urth in the sky?"

"Oh, that's easy," Margie laughed, for she'd already figured it out. "We're on the 'back side' of Lunera, the side never facing Urth. And since no one on Urth can see us, we can't see Urth either."

The nerva blinked its red eyes in sudden understanding. "Why, of course!" it cried. "Why didn't I think of that before? I'm astonished at your clever mind, Margie. You're destined for greatness."

Margie grinned and the nerva said, "It's time to go home. You and Hal climb onto my back. I'm going to fly us there."

"But what about the other children?" Hal piped up. "What will happen to them?"

"Don't worry. They're free now. There are other nervas on this moon, trapped like me, who will fly them back to Urth. Thanks to you, Auntie has no more power to hold children, or nervas, captive anymore."

Thus assured, Margie and Hal hopped on and clung tight to the back of the nerva as it flew straight up the bank of windows and through an opening under the eaves.

Up, up, up they went, leaving the castle far below, until it was just a tiny dot. Then the nerva flew them east for hundreds of miles until they emerged from the "back side" of Lunera and could see Urth, their home, a beautiful sight, bright blue against an inky background speckled with distant stars.

It was just a few minutes, then, before Margie and Hal were back in their ducky sacks, safe once more as if nothing had happened, far from the sorceress and her evil doings.

"Good-bye, nerva!" they cried in unison as the creature (now back to its usual size) flew away. As it went, it waved a grateful wing in their direction.

Margie and Hal prospered after that and grew into fine young people, choosing adult "renames" for themselves, as all Urth children do, scrambling around the letters in their birth names, a tradition as old as the dawn of time.

Hal became Ahl, a highly regarded artist, while Margie, now Mirage, trained under the great astronomer Axerladen Fiddle and became Urth's most respected astronomer of the time, as great in reputation as she

*They emerged from the "back side" of Lunera and could see Urth, their home, bright blue against an inky background speckled with distant stars...*

was in height. Indeed, a famous sculptor created her likeness, and the statue stood for centuries until the Great Melt finally washed it away.

Such is the tale of two Urth children, who were moonslings for a while. And, although they enjoyed moonsgazing at the "front side" of Lunera for the rest of their lives, they never forgot their time on the "back side," hidden from view.

Indeed, every dark and moons-less night, they recalled the terror of being snatched from their ducky sacks. They remembered Auntie, her castle, and the scary orange light of an enormous Ru.

And *ooh...* they shivered!

# 2

# East Basin and the Paddling Games

*In which a young herdsman's "deformity" becomes a great advantage.*

I n the days before your grandmother was a girl, and even before your grandmother's grandmother's grandfather walked Urth, there lived a boy named Sebastian Kaya, who tended a fine herd of "palaca" on his Uncle Yar's farm in the high mountains of the great continent of Urt.

In those early times, there were several continents on

*The gentle palaca of Urt...*

Urth, but Urt was the largest. It sprawled hundreds of miles west to east, and hundreds of miles north to south, teeming with strange and wonderful animals like palaca. The palaca were gentle creatures with soft, durable wool, and artisans spun it into "pal," a warm, watertight fabric ideal for clothing.

Back then, Urth's climate was chillier than it is today. In the region of Urt where Sebastian lived, the winters were long and hard. When the snow came, it buried the land. The cozy, vibrant tunics and dresses, fashioned from pal, helped people survive in body and spirit until the world thawed again and the brilliant blue skies and rich green "head grass" returned to the high hills.

Sebastian's job was to make sure that their herd ate plenty of this life-nourishing grass, moving the beasts from one high grazing pasture to the next all summer long, until the animals' wool reached its full glory and was ready for market in the village far below. Sebastian enjoyed shearing the palaca, removing long strips of their heavy wool until the animals were bald and looked silly.

Like the good guardian that he was, Yar drilled into Sebastian how important the palaca were for their survival.

"When the palaca eat well in the summers, we eat well in the winters. But if the palaca starve, so do we."

Sebastian knew that his uncle was right. Wool from a well-fed palaca fetched a much higher price than wool from a poorly fed one. When they sold the wool, they used the money for necessities like firewood and potatoes. Therefore, Sebastian took his work seriously, keeping an eye on the herd at all times, making sure his charges were shoulder-deep in fine head grass all summer long.

Herding was not difficult work. Palaca were sociable, friendly animals that liked to stay together. When one of them strayed, Sebastian tooted on his whistle, and it returned. What's more, there were no predators in the mountains of Urt for Sebastian to worry about, no carnivores lurking in the high grass waiting to pounce. In truth, his job was easy, and often rather boring, giving him plenty of time to think.

*Sebastian had plenty of time to think...*

"Why does Uncle Yar keep me so isolated?" he often wondered, as he gazed down at the herd. "I'm not a child anymore. I'm growing up. My hair is long and thick. My muscles are strong. I could take the wool to market on his behalf. He's getting old, and the journey is hard for him. But he keeps me a prisoner up here in the hills. I'm so lonely. I want to see the world beyond the Kaya farm. I want to see the faraway ocean that I read about in books. I want to meet other people and have a *real* life."

Sebastian didn't keep these thoughts to himself. In the evenings, he peppered his uncle with questions, and, the older he grew, the more insistent and frequent they became.

"Uncle, you *must* let me venture past the rickety gate that separates our farm from the rest of Urt! Why do you refuse? I'll be choosing a 'rename' soon, and after that I'll be able to make my own decisions. Renaming is a tradition as old as our two moons, Lunera and Ru. I will scramble the letters in 'Sebastian' to choose a new name of my own. You can't keep me here forever."

His uncle's response was always the same.

"You can leave when you're older. I'll answer your questions when the time is right. Meanwhile, enjoy what's left of your childhood. It will never come again, and, once you leave the safe world I've created for you, your life won't be the same. Trust me when I say this."

Sebastian had to obey his elders until he renamed himself, and he couldn't rename himself until he hit puberty. It seemed an eternity as he waited for his voice to deepen and his body to mature, but the day for his Renaming Ceremony finally came, and he chose the adult name East Basin, leaving the boy Sebastian behind forever. East Basin was a real place, far away, famous for its wildflower blooms in early spring. One day, he hoped to travel to the wondrous valley and see it for himself. By taking the name East Basin, he hoped his dream would come true.

"I'm going to take the wool to the village tomorrow," he announced to his uncle that evening. "It's my Renaming Wish, and you can't deny it. It's the law of the land."

Yar knew this was true, drawing in a deep breath.

"I understand," he replied, his eyes full of sorrow. "You're an adult now, not a child. But I grew up in that village, and it's a terrible place for the likes of us. That's why I brought you up here to the mountains, where we could be alone. You won't be welcome in the world beyond this farm. If you go to the village tomorrow, you'll regret it."

East Basin frowned.

"Uncle, I've had enough of your mysterious hints. I need to know the truth about why you've kept me here. I'm going to the village tomorrow, whether you like it or not, and I want to know what I'm facing."

Seeing he had no choice, Yar buried his face in his hands.

East Basin leaned over and put an arm around him. He loved his uncle, even though he was sometimes frustrated with him. Clearly, whatever was haunting him was difficult to bear.

"Tell me," he urged gently, squatting at his uncle's side. "I know it's hard for you. I can see you're deeply ashamed of something. But whatever your secret is, please don't keep it from me any longer. I'd rather learn the truth from you than learn it from strangers."

Yar looked up, his eyes wet with tears.

"It's the Kaya Curse," he said, his voice breaking. "When you get to the village, people will gawk, but you must learn to ignore them. They know the Kayas produce the finest palaca wool in the region, and they will always buy it, even though we are deformed and unfit for their company."

East Basin frowned and cocked his head to one side, confused.

"Deformed? What do you mean? There's nothing wrong with us."

"Oh, yes there is. I know you'll find it hard to believe, but it's true. It's a family defect, going back many generations. You see, many of us Kayas, including you and me, have webbing between our fingers. I know it seems normal to you. You've never known any different. But it's a deformity out there in the wider world."

East Basin couldn't hide his astonishment. Like all Urth people, he had webbed feet. His distant ancestors had evolved by the sea after all. But he'd always assumed that other people had webbed hands, too.

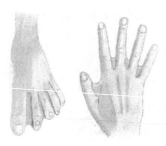

*East Basin's hands and feet*

"You mean most people *don't* have webbed hands?" he asked incredulously. "Really? I can't imagine it."

"No, they *don't*," Yar sobbed. "They have long,

slender fingers disconnected from one another. We Kayas are different from the rest. We're ugly."

East Basin was shocked. It had never entered his mind that he was ugly, nor that he had a curse. No wonder his uncle had kept him on the farm! What loving guardian wouldn't have done the same? He suddenly understood his uncle like never before, and was sorry he'd ever doubted him. Compassion rushed into his heart and tears welled in his eyes. How deeply his uncle had suffered!

"I'll stay here," East Basin said, prepared to give up his dream of seeing the world. "I'll remain here forever, by your side."

"No, no. You must go to the village and see the truth for yourself before you decide what to do," Yar told him. "You have a yearning to see the world, and, if you don't go tomorrow you'll go another day. Keep to your plan, and take the wool to market. We'll talk when you get home."

After a restless night's sleep, East Basin woke at dawn and threw a halter over the family's faithful "macel," strapping the animal to a cart stacked with bundles of palaca wool.

He was scared, but also excited. He was leaving the Kaya farm at last! As the family's faithful

*East Basin threw a halter over the family's faithful macel...*

macel trotted him through the countryside, his heart
soared. When he entered the woods that ran along the
river, he gasped with delight. He pulled the macel to a
halt and hopped off, gazing in jaw-dropped wonder at
the tall trees. He'd never been in a forest before. It was
an alien world. The highlands were devoid of all but
scrubby bushes that offered no shade.

East Basin wandered around the woods for a while,
but eventually returned to his macel and cart to resume
his journey. He clattered across a bridge and emerged
from the forest, finding himself on the outskirts of the
town. There, he met a peasant, who was leading a stout
"gip" along the road, gripping the ring in its nose to
keep it on course. Gips were much like pigs. Urth people prized them for their meat, and most families in the
village kept a few.

Despite holing him away, Yar had educated his nephew
well. He'd cleverly excised portions of the pictures from
the books in their library so East Basin wouldn't see "normal" hands. Nonetheless, East Basin instantly recognized
the peasant for who she was: a young woman. He glanced,
briefly, at her hands, with their separated, bony fingers,
which (to him) looked odd, indeed. But he didn't allow his
gaze to linger there. Instead, he gave her a hearty greeting.

He cried, "Good morning, Miss! How are you this
lovely day?"

She smiled. In a small town like hers, a new face
(and a handsome one at that) was always welcome. She

wondered who he was and where he was going.

She was about to bid him a good morning, too, but the words died in her mouth. The young man's cart, she suddenly noticed, was heavy with palaca wool. That could only mean one thing.

She pulled in her breath sharply.

"You have the Kaya Curse," she cried, nearly tripping over her gip as she backed away. "Don't come any closer to me or I'll scream!"

East Basin's smile vanished as the woman slapped her gip on the flanks and hurried after the annoyed animal as it trotted quickly in the opposite direction. Both of them soon disappeared around a bend, the woman's grass-colored skirt merging with the rustling green of the river rushes.

East Basin sat down in his saddle and took up the reins again.

"I hope the other villagers aren't so afraid of me," he thought.

A little further along, he passed a group of boys who were a few years younger than he was. At first, they were friendly, too. But when they noticed the wool in his cart, their attitude changed.

One of them shouted, "You're old man Kaya's nephew, come down from the high hills at last. We know about you! You've got the Kaya Curse."

Another boy picked up a rock and held it high, ready to strike.

He jeered, "Go to market and sell your palaca wool. Stay away from us!"

East Basin's heart sank, but he didn't let the boys see how hurt he was. Though his face burned with embarrassment and his eyes stung with hot tears, he kept the cart moving.

Once he reached the village, East Basin wasn't quite sure where to go. But an old woman in a yellow scarf (made from fine pal, he noticed) pointed her bony index finger in the right direction.

"That's where folks like *you* go," she said sharply. Then she disappeared down the street in a rush, holding up her skirts as she ran.

Mortified now, and pulling his sleeves down over his hands in shame, East Basin found the Kaya booth and laid out the wool. People queued up to buy it, too, one right after the other, as his uncle had predicted. But even as they fingered the wool and "oohed" and "ahhed" over its excellence, they kept their distance and never allowed their children to get near.

"Infectious," he heard one of the women hiss at her son. "Stay away."

The morning dragged on, and by noon East Basin was feeling so humiliated that he began to pack up and leave the market before all the wool was sold. But before he could complete his task, a young man approached him. He was fit and lean, and only a few years older than East Basin. He seemed very anxious to make his acquaintance.

He asked eagerly, "You're a Kaya, aren't you? A man selling apples a few stalls down pointed you out."

East Basin eyed the man warily. Given his treatment thus far, he steeled himself. He waited for the man to say something nasty.

Instead, once the man had learned East Basin's name, and confirmed the Kaya connection, he introduced himself in turn, holding out his hand.

He said, "I'm Coach Osman and I know all about your so-called 'curse.' Join hands with me and you'll see that I'm a friend, not a foe."

East Basin cautiously complied, and when Coach Osman shook his hand without a trace of fear or disgust, his fear eased and he relaxed.

"I run the Phantom Sharks paddling team in New Harbor Town, many hundreds of miles from here, on the western shores of the Eastern Sea," Coach Osman explained. "I need new talent. My team is one boy short. If I don't recruit another one, the Sharks can't compete this season. I heard about your family and have come a long way."

"I'm a Kaya, all right, and I have plenty of palaca wool to sell—the finest in this part of the country. Did you really come hundreds of miles to buy it?"

"Buy your wool? No, that's not my mission," Coach Osman assured him, with a light laugh. "You misunderstand my intent. I've come to *recruit* you. I need you for the Phantom Sharks. You're different from the rest and have a great advantage. You're built for sport paddling. I think you're just the boy I need."

To say the least, East Basin wasn't expecting this.

"I don't understand," he said.

"I'll bet you don't," Coach Osman replied with a smile. "Look here. Some folks are frightened of people who are different. But I'm not like them. When I look at you, I don't see a boy with a curse. I see a lucky young man who has *four* webbed appendages, not just two. I see a natural born athlete made for sport paddling. What do you say?"

East Basin knew all about sport paddling. It involved a ball, a net, and swimmers competing to make goals.

"You want *me* to play for the Phantom Sharks?" he cried, scarcely believing his ears. The team was famous. News traveled to the village, and Yar brought the *Village Times* home every week. East Basin was aware of the team's reputation and was stunned that such an offer would come to him, of all people.

"But I've never paddled in my life. The lake on our farm is only a foot deep, and that's in the rainy season."

"You'll learn," Coach Osman assured him. "It won't take long. All Urth people can paddle. It's in our nature. I've trained many mountain boys before. You'll be surprised how quickly you take to it."

East Basin nearly jumped for joy. Had he lived alone, he'd have followed Coach Osman back to New Harbor Town immediately. *The western shore of the Eastern Sea.*

*The Phantom Sharks!* But East Basin needed to think of his uncle. Even though he could legally make his own decisions, he recognized his responsibility. The poor man had no one else to rely upon, and, with the Kaya Curse, he never would.

He said reluctantly, "I can't. I live with my uncle who's too old to herd the palaca and keep them healthy and shorn. There's no one else to help him. I'm his only family."

Coach Osman considered this dilemma but plowed ahead, anyway. He'd been scouting new talent for several months, and he needed a full team of skilled players. As it was, the Sharks had only seven. The sport required eight. He did not want the team disqualified from competition, but he wasn't willing to lower his standards, either. He was ambitious for the Sharks, and would search high and low to find a boy who could not only fill out the team, but make it better.

After a few moments, he replied, "I think we can work this out. It's the end of the shearing season now, isn't it? The snows are coming, and your uncle won't need you to take the animals out again until next spring. Let me come home with you and speak with him. When he hears my proposition, I think he'll agree."

Coach Osman was right. When East Basin broke the news to Yar and explained the coach's plans for him, everything clicked into place. Coach Osman, it turned out, was a distant cousin, in a branch of the Kaya family tree that didn't have the Kaya Curse. Yar could see that he was a good man who could be trusted with the welfare of his nephew.

"It's not my choice whether you go or not," Yar reminded East Basin. "But if it were, I'd advise you to go. Go to the western shore of the Eastern Sea and play for the Phantom Sharks."

"But what about the winter? How will you weather it alone?"

*Coach Osman produced a sack of golden tidbits...*

"This will help," Coach Osman interrupted, retrieving a sack of golden "tidbits" from inside his tunic. "We pay the families of our players. It's compensation for taking their young men away from home for months at a time."

East Basin whooped with delight. The worst day in his life had suddenly become his best, and he couldn't contain his excitement. With the coins in the mix, the last vestiges of worry for his uncle's welfare evaporated. With that kind of money, Yar would have no trouble making it through the winter in ease and comfort.

Coach Osman spent the night. The next morning, he helped East Basin pack his few belongings for the journey.

"Thank you, uncle," East Basin said gratefully, as he paused in the doorway and gave him a long hug. "I hope you're not too lonely while I'm gone. I'll miss you."

"I doubt you'll miss me much," Yar laughed, shooing

East Basin along. "You'll be seeing the world instead. But if you think of it, write to me now and then. I want to hear all about your adventures while I await your return."

The journey from the high mountains of Urt to the western shores of the Eastern Sea was arduous, but worth it. When East Basin arrived and experienced the rapture of paddling for the first time, his spirit soared in utter ecstasy. Under the bright light of Lunera, the larger and brighter of Urth's two moons, he plunged

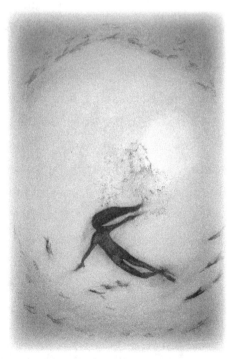

*Under the bright light of Lunera,*
*he plunged into the cool depths...*

into the cool depths, and, as he merged with the salty water, his webbed feet and hands naturally widened out and surged him forward. Coach Osman was right. He was born to paddle!

At first, the boys on the Phantom Sharks team welcomed him, delighted that their coach had recruited an eighth player. Soon, however, they noticed his unusual hands, and while most were more curious than afraid, the eldest grew quiet and his eyes darkened.

"Knock it off, Ahdem," Coach Osman chided him. "East Basin's hands are a great advantage. With him on board, the Phantom Sharks will win many paddling competitions this season. We might even make it to the Paddling Games! But we've got to pull together if we're to do it."

Ahdem respected his coach, but he was accustomed to being the top player on the team. On the outside, he pretended to cooperate, but inwardly he fumed. During the day's practice, as East Basin's superior speed in the water became apparent, he grew more and more angry.

"It's not *fair*," he told himself. "East Basin's new to the game, but soon he'll be paddling faster than me. Wait until I tell my father about this. He'll do something about it!"

Ahdem's father was troubled to hear the news. In fact, he was more outraged than his son.

He barked, "A boy with webbed hands? I learned about that deformity in school. The Kaya Curse, they call it. How can Coach Osman justify recruiting such a boy for the Phantom Sharks? He might as well have recruited a sea creature, complete with fins and gills. *Swish swish!* I'll take this up with him tomorrow and put an end to this nonsense."

Sure enough, the next morning, Ahdem's father confronted Coach Osman at the paddling arena, where the boys were practicing.

"What's this I hear about a boy with the Kaya Curse playing for the Phantom Sharks?" he growled. "You know it's wrong. A boy like that isn't natural."

"I don't see it that way," Coach Osman replied, in an even tone. "In fact, I believe just the opposite. East Basin's exceptional hands are great for the team, and I have no intention of sending him home to the high mountains of Urt where his talent would wither in the head grass."

"Well, if you don't see the bias in all this, the Paddling Games Commission will. Mark my words! They make the final decisions about such matters, and I intend to take the matter up with them."

True to his word, Ahdem's father lodged a formal complaint against the coach with the Commission that afternoon.

As the head of the Paddling Games Commission listened to Ahdem's father spout off about injustice, she grew worried. He was a wealthy, well-connected politician. If he demanded an investigation into the situation, she'd have to give him one.

She talked matters over with the other members of the Commission the next day, and they scheduled a hearing for the following Sunday, open to the paddling team parents, East Basin, and Coach Osman (the accused).

Hearings were no light matter. They were legal proceedings, and, as the day approached, East Basin grew silent and sullen. The entire focus of the proceedings would be on *him*, and his *deformity*. He regretted the day he'd met Coach Osman and agreed to join the team.

"I'm going home," he decided. "My uncle is right. The only safe place for the likes of me is the Kaya farm."

He told Coach Osman what he planned to do, but the coach rebuffed him.

"I know your family has suffered, but hiding only makes things worse. You don't have to testify. I'll do all the talking in my own defense. Try to relax if you can."

On Sunday morning, Coach Osman led a reluctant East Basin to the courthouse. By the time they arrived, all the seats (except the two reserved for them) were full. Every parent of a Phantom Sharks team member was present. They stared at the newcomer angrily. By then, word had gotten around about "the Kaya kid," and Ahdem's father had rallied everyone to his side.

Coach Osman and East Basin took their seats near the front of the chamber, directly in front of the Commission panel and the witness stand. East Basin didn't dare look behind him, at the glowering crowd, though he could feel their eyes burning into the back of his skull. Instinctively, he pulled down his shirtsleeves to cover his hands.

After the "court crier" had read the charges against Coach Osman, the head of the Commission called the first witness to testify: Ahdem's father.

As expected, the powerful man exuded righteous indignation and made no bones about his position on the matter before the court.

"Ahdem's been a member of the Phantom Sharks for three years," he snarled, "and he's the best player of the bunch. Now, Coach Osman has recruited this young upstart, with the Kaya Curse no less, to join the team. It's unfair to the other players. Why, just look at him. He's afraid to show his hands!"

Ahdem's father pointed directly at East Basin, who wanted to wither up and die.

The crowd murmured its agreement.

Coach Osman rose and strolled to the witness booth until he was only a few feet away from Ahdem's father. The man stared at him, threateningly, but Coach Osman smiled pleasantly, as if they were discussing the weather.

"Your son's a great player," he agreed. "He works hard at practice and is highly skilled. The team is lucky to have him."

Ahdem's father was somewhat mollified. He liked hearing his son praised, and he lifted his nose in pride.

A few "hear, hears!" erupted from the audience, but the head of the Commission called for silence.

"I'll tolerate no interruptions," she cautioned the crowd sternly. "This is a serious business. Coach Osman's career is at stake. Any more outbursts, and I'll throw you all out."

The chamber went silent, and she gestured for Coach Osman to continue, which he did.

"Yes, Ahdem is an exceptional player. He puts his whole heart into the game. He's also several inches taller than the other players, which helps the team a lot. Unusually tall, just like you."

Ahdem's father puffed up. He enjoyed being lofty and imposing. It helped him boss other people about.

He agreed with a nod, "That's right. Ahdem's tall, all right."

*Ahdem could leap higher than the rest of the boys...*

Coach Osman cast a sidelong glance at the head of the Paddling Games Commission, who was watching with interest. "Exactly. It gives him a real edge, doesn't it?"

"It does. He can leap higher out of the water and catch the ball far more easily than any other player."

Coach Osman said, "I see. But isn't that unfair to the other players, who don't have his height? Perhaps I should remove Ahdem from the team. Yes, I think it's the right thing to do."

Ahdem's father was livid. Coach Osman had maneuvered him into a corner, and he suddenly realized he'd been trapped.

"But you *can't* do that!" he cried.

Coach Osman replied, "Yes, I can. As long as I lead this team, it's my decision to make."

Ahdem's father rose from his seat and shot back a nasty remark about the Commission having the power to remove him from his post, but the head of the Commission put up a finger to silence him.

"Next witness," she said, after a short deliberation with one of her colleagues. "Let's see what the other parents have to say."

Mila's mother came to the stand next, her face grim with determination. She was an aggressive woman who ruled her household with an iron fist, including her frail husband, who cowered in her presence.

"Mila is an excellent player, too," she cried the moment she took her seat. "Ahdem's not the only top boy!"

Coach Osman was well prepared and approached her with a portrait of Mila, held up high.

"Yes. That's true," he agreed. "Mila practices all the time. He's earned his spot on the team, no doubt about it."

Mila's mother relaxed. She'd trained her son to take the sport seriously. She took Coach Osman's compliment as a praise of her mothering abilities.

The coach continued, "And he's an unusual boy, too. Like all of us, he has a thin layer of blubber around his midsection to keep him buoyant and warm while paddling. But your son's blubber is pale, not the usual deep indigo. I believe you have the same trait, madam. Would you mind displaying it to the court?"

Mila's mother got to her feet and proudly lifted the hem of her blouse. People in her region prized pale blubber and she enjoyed showing it off.

Her demeanor softened. "Yes, it runs in our family. Mila inherited it, as did my daughter Zura."

"Yes, I see. And what a wonderful trait it is for a sport paddler! Mila can slip past the defensive line more easily than the other players. They have trouble seeing him."

"That's right," she replied proudly, walking straight into the same trap Coach Osman had set for Ahdem's father.

"But also unfair to the other players, I think," Coach Osman added, raising an eyebrow. "Perhaps I should remove Mila from the team. It seems like the right thing to do."

Mila's mother grew irate and lifted a finger in her son's defense, ready to protest, but the head of the Commission stopped her in her tracks.

"Step down, Ma'am," she ordered. "Your testimony is done."

Somewhat deflated, she vacated the stand, replaced by the father of a boy named Brek. He was a happy-go-lucky fellow, and Coach Osman made quick work of him.

"What do you think of the hearing so far?" the coach asked.

"Well, maybe you're right about Ahdem and Mila," he admitted, with a shrug. "But my Brek is on the up and up. Pure talent, that one."

Coach Osman walked to a nearby window and opened it. The breeze lifted the curtains.

He said, "A bit hot today, don't you agree? So toasty that we're not wearing our turbans."

Brek's father smiled.

"The heat doesn't bother me," he chuckled. "I'm bald."

Coach Osman nodded.

"I can see that. And I believe your son is bald as well."

"Yup. He is."

"Hmmm..." Coach Osman responded. "That makes Brek different from his friends. Does it make him feel like an odd man out?"

*Brek's father was bald...*

"A bit," Brek's father admitted. "When he was younger, perhaps. But once he found sport paddling, all that changed."

"Is that so?" Coach Osman asked, laying his bait.

"Oh, yes. No hair, no real estate for the other players to grab onto to block a pass. Once he figured that out, he was glad he was bald."

"But isn't it true," Coach Osman continued, "that sport paddlers aren't permitted to shave their heads? The game's rules forbid it. Yet your son has no hair and he's still allowed to compete."

"Yes, but the rule doesn't apply to him, you see," Brek's father responded, clearly amused with the direction his testimony was taking. "He doesn't have any hair to begin with."

Coach Osman replied, "How interesting. I'm just wondering, though. Why should a rule apply to every boy on a team but one? It seems decidedly unfair. It never occurred to me before, but now that charges have been brought against me, I see things more clearly."

Renac's mother was next. She'd arrived at the hearing just as vexed as the others, but now she seemed unsure of her position.

As she took her seat, she muttered uncertainly, "My son is just an *ordinary* boy." Then she looked pleadingly at the head of the Paddling Games Commission and added, "Isn't he?"

Coach Osman approached her with laugh and a shake of his head.

"Renac is the smartest thing on two legs," he pointed out, reminding her of all the academic awards her son had earned in school. "He can figure out the playbooks of the opposing team in less than ten seconds and rally all the other players around him. He's indispensable to the team, the very brain of the outfit. But perhaps—and I'm just thinking aloud here—his unusual intelligence puts him in a different league from the others. If I were the parent of a boy who worked hard but didn't have your son's intelligence, I might be upset."

"Well, when you put it that way," she murmured reluctantly, "I guess Renac *is* above the rest. I never thought about it like that."

Mec's father was the last to testify, but the fight was completely out of him. Instead of defending his son, he bragged about him instead.

"Mec can hold his breath for nearly an hour. Twice as long as most Urth people. I can do the same, and so have the men in our family for many generations back. If you want to boot him off the team for it, I think you're a fool."

Mec's father left the witness stand, and Coach Osman approached the Commission. A defendant was the one who called witnesses, and he was done.

"I have no more witnesses," he informed them. "My fate as a coach, and East Basin's future as a player, is up to you."

At the defense table, East Basin was in a muddle. Every ounce of his being wanted to flee the room. If the Commission ruled against Coach Osman, they'd both be banned from the sport. Even worse, it would confirm, in a most public way, that the Kaya Curse was a deformity that disqualified a person from a rightful place in society.

"I don't care about myself," East Basin thought determinedly. "I can go back to my uncle and the life I had before. But I can't stand to see Coach Osman lose his job. He's so good at what he does, and he took a chance on me."

Thus, East Basin made a decision that would change his life forever. In a feat of almost unbelievable bravery, he pulled back his shirtsleeves and exposed his hands to the harsh glare of the lights of the room. Spreading out his fingers, he exposed the unusual webbing, for all to see.

"There you go!" he thought, catching the eyes of several members of the Commission. "There's the 'deformity' that everyone's so worried about."

Coach Osman's eyes widened. He stared at East Basin in awe.

"What guts," he thought gratefully. "What a courageous heart. I do believe this boy will be my salvation!"

There was a moment of silence as the members of the Commission stared at East Basin's hands. They'd never seen the Kaya Curse for themselves. Somehow, they'd imagined that East Basin's hands would resemble those of a duck. Instead, the delicate webbing was rather unremarkable. It would help him paddle, no doubt, but why all the fuss?

The members of the Commission nodded at Coach Osman and East Basin. Then they collectively rose from their seats and left the room.

It didn't take them long to arrive at their decision and announce it to the restless crowd. Given the proceedings, they felt secure in their position. They were no longer worried about Ahdem's father and his political influence. The parents were with them now.

"Coach Osman, please rise," the head of the Commission said, meeting his eyes with deep respect. "Our decision is that you're cleared of all charges. You've convinced us, today, that all the boys on the team, including East Basin, are important members. Each is different from the others, with a great advantage of his own. These natural gifts, along with their hard work, is what makes the Phantom Sharks so strong. You've done an excellent job recruiting the boys, and we wish you a successful season!"

The Phantom Sharks won the Paddling Games that year. The Commission voted East Basin Most Valuable Player, and when he went home to the mountains of Urt in the early spring, a hero, the children of the village gathered around and followed him back to his uncle's house.

"How can we get Kaya hands?" they asked eagerly. "You're a great sport paddler and we want to be just like you."

Yar grinned from ear to ear. The deformity that had haunted and isolated his family for so many generations was now a matter of celebrity! There would be no more hiding, for there was nothing to hide.

"It's time to sell the farm," he thought. "East Basin has a career now and can support us both. I'll retire and move to New Harbor Town. It will be fun to follow the Phantom Sharks from game to game and root them on."

East Basin played for the team for five more seasons, thrice leading his teammates to glory in the Paddling Games. Then, he married Mila's lovely sister, Zura, and settled down, working as Coach Osman's assistant coach and talent scout.

East Basin didn't have to look far for the next great player. As fate would have it, his own son Sai got twice lucky, inheriting both his mother's pale blubber *and* his father's webbed hands.

What's more, surrounded by people who celebrated his natural differences, Sai was able to make the most of them, leading the Phantom Sharks into a golden era where they dominated the sport for ten years straight, never losing a single game. For Sai had *two* great advantages, not just one, and that made his team stronger than ever.

# 3

# The Poison Well

*In which a quiet, watchful boy becomes a hero.*

On an Urth island called Fall Oran, a very long time ago, there once stood a village called Curimicu, surrounded on all sides by a dense forest.

The chance that you've heard of Curimicu is next to none. Even Urth children know little about it, because the last person to remember the last person who remembered the last person, who remembered anyone in the village is long since dead. But I know what happened in that village, because I recently discovered a scroll, written by a boy named Bai, that describes it all in great detail. And, as you'll soon see, it was a lucky find, for it's important to know what happened in Curimicu, so it doesn't happen to you.

Bai was a quiet child and listened well. With his keen black eyes wide open, he watched what the people of

*Bai wrote the story down on a scroll...*

Curimicu did. He was too young for the villagers to take seriously, but was the wisest of them all, for he sensed something that none of them did: *the danger of the Land for All.*

The Land for All was a large, green fertile field with excellent soil and tall, nutritious grass for grazing, with a well at the center that brimmed with sweet spring water there for the taking. The villagers' houses populated this abundant place of plenty, ten of them together in a circle, with the Land for All in the middle. And in each house there lived ten people, none as wise as Bai.

When Bai's family moved to the village, it hadn't existed for very long. Fifteen years before, a hunter had emerged from the surrounding forest, and happened upon the rich land by accident, with its little well in the middle. He could see the potential of the place, and, being a man of action, he decided to settle down there immediately.

*There was a little well in the middle of the rich land...*

"I'll start a village here," he proclaimed, "and give it my family name." So Mil Curimicu staked out his claim, as they did in those days, by pounding four stakes into the ground. The land was free for the owning, and he was prepared to share it with all who wished to come.

Mil wasn't married, and his parents fumed and stewed about it, because they wanted grandchildren. When he wrote them a letter and told them about his good fortune, they immediately sent him a young woman to be his bride. Her name was Mi Ling, and she was quite lovely, so Mil agreed to marry her. Five years later, they had eight sons under their roof, including a set of quadruplets.

The woman who chaperoned Mi Ling to Mil's new village decided to settle there, too. Her husband had died and left her with nine children and she had nowhere else to go. Mil helped her build a house of her own, and then there were two families in the village, with ten people each, mostly children.

Five years later, the village was flourishing, with nine huts, each with ten people. And every house had domestic animals called "wocs" and "gips," with woc-itties (woc babies) and gipitties (gip babies) born until each family had five of each.

"It's wonderful in Curimicu," Bai's father told his family when they entered the village for the first time. "There's a common land, with plenty for everyone, that has abundant grass and a well in the middle. We're

*Every house had wocs and gips...*

going to live in this village from now on. I'm going to buy a woc and gip to get us started."

Then he built their cottage, which became the tenth of the bunch, and a barn for the livestock.

Bai was old enough to help with the animals, so his father put him to work, explaining that they must limit the numbers of gips and wocs they kept.

"The other villagers have only five wocs and five gips apiece, and we need to fit in."

Bai's father detailed his plan further.

"You'll take our woc into the Land for All, and make her good and fat. Then we'll mate her to a male woc, and she'll have a litter of four wocitties. After that, we'll have five wocs in all. Then, each time a woc gives birth, we'll slaughter another for food.

"And you'll journey to the well each day, and collect fresh, pure water for our gip. Then we'll mate her to a male gip, and she'll have a litter of four gipitties. After that, we'll have five gips altogether. Each time a gip gives birth, we'll slaughter another for food. Then we'll prosper, like our neighbors, and there will be no more hunger in our family."

Bai did as he was told, and within a few years, their hard work paid off. They had five healthy wocs and five lively gips. What's more, Bai's mother gave birth to an eighth

*Yei Min had watchful black eyes...*

child, a little girl named Yei Min, whom Bai loved in a way he didn't love the others. Bai took her under his wing, as they had much in common. Unlike the rest of his siblings, who were rowdy and loud, Yei-Min was quiet and curious, with watchful black eyes just like his.

The trouble began around the time Bai first noticed hairs sprouting above his upper lip. One day, when he was grazing the family's five wocs, he noticed that one was getting fat around the middle. This was happy news, and when he arrived home that evening, he announced the good tidings at dinner.

"One of the wocs is pregnant."

Bai's father was pleased. It meant they could slaughter a woc soon and his family would eat well in the following weeks.

But Bai's mother shrugged off Bai's news, offering

an unexpected, alternative plan.

She said, "We don't need to slaughter a woc. Two houses down, the Hing family has six. I hear all the gossip in the village, you know, and it's true. What's more, they handle six just fine. They only slaughter a woc when they have seven. They use up a bit more of the rich grass in the Land for All now, but there's plenty to spare."

"Then we will have six wocs, too," replied Bai's father. "If the Hings do it, so can we. It's important to keep up with our neighbors." Thus, when their woc give birth to its fine wocitty, he didn't slaughter another. The sixth woc appeared to have no negative impact on the Land for All and meant only a minor increase in their workload.

Bai had an uneasy feeling about the sixth woc. It nagged at him, but not knowing why, he didn't say anything to his parents. Instead, he confessed his anxiety to Yei Min as they lay in their "ducky sacks," the cozy, feather-filled comforters they used for bedding.

"Little sister, once there were fifty wocs grazing in the Land for All and now there are fifty-two. I don't know why this upsets me, but it does."

"We'll understand one day," she replied, "for we hear and see much, you and I. Let's wait a few Ru months and see what happens."

Urth has two moons, Lunera and Ru, and thus two different kinds of months. The people of Curimicu, however, followed Ru months more closely. Thus, Bai kept his eye on the sky, following the orange moon as it cycled through it's phases. Sure enough, exactly four Ru months later, Bai noticed that one of the gips was getting fat around the middle, too.

When he realized what was happening, he informed his father, "One of the gips is pregnant."

Bai's father smiled. "We can slaughter a gip soon," he said, "and we'll have bacon for breakfast."

Bai's mother disagreed.

She said, "There's no need to slaughter a gip. Three huts down, the Eel family has six gips. I hear all the gossip in the village, you know, and this is true. What's more, they manage just fine. They take a little more water from the well each day, but there's plenty to spare."

"Then I suppose we should do the same," Bai's father replied. "The more gips we keep, the more bacon we'll have in the future."

Once more, Bai kept quiet, sharing his growing doubt with Yei Min.

"Once there were fifty gips drinking water from the well and soon there will be fifty-two. I don't know why this upsets me, but it does."

"We'll understand one day," she replied, "for we hear and see much, you and I."

A few more Ru months passed, and Bai noticed something else.

"Mrs. Chung has moved the wall of her garden," he

*Bai's mother wanted room for a coop...*

pointed out to his mother one morning. "It's poking out now, into the Land for All. Her yard is bigger than anyone else's."

She replied, "I noticed that, and I've decided we need a bigger garden, too. I want to raise some 'ne-chicks' and we need room for a coop."

Bai frowned and, for the first time, expressed his concerns with her.

Tentatively he said, "If everyone expands their properties, the Land for All will grow smaller and smaller, don't you think?"

"I suppose so," she countered. "But there's enough for everyone. Look around you. Remember when all the families in this village had only five wocs and five gips? Well, now everyone has six of each. Yet the Land for

All hasn't suffered one bit, has it? The grass is healthy
and abundant. The water in the well is flowing pure and
clean, the same as always."

Bai had to admit this was true. The Land for All
appeared as robust as ever. When he crawled into bed
beside his sister that night, he mumbled, "Why am I so
troubled?"

A few more Ru months galloped by, and Bai's mother
built a spacious coop, filling it with ten ne-chicks.

One morning she said with satisfaction, "Now we'll
have eggs to eat every morning. Just like the Chungs."

Bai had to admit that the eggs were a nice addition
to the family's diet, but he couldn't fully enjoy them.
After a while, he stopped eating them altogether.

Worried that Bai was ill, his parents called in a doctor to examine him.

"It's nothing serious," the doctor declared, washing
up after the examination. "He has a high-strung temperament, that's all. He thinks too much. Perhaps you should
send him away to school. I think he'll prosper there."

Bai's parents discussed the matter and decided it
was the right thing to do. So they sent Bai to a faraway
city in the south, where they had a distant relative who
was willing to take him in and help with the costs of
his education.

Bai was happy at school, studied hard, and learned

to read and write, unlike the villagers back home, who were illiterate.

"You're a bright boy," the headmaster praised him one hot summer's day. "Though you don't say much in class, you do well on your exams. You've earned a trip home if you want to go. You've been away from your family for more than a year. I'll lend you a fast 'sehor' for your journey."

Sehors were much like horses, and Bai had learned to ride at school. He leapt at the chance to go home and see Yei Min, and galloped off the next morning.

When he approached Curimicu, and called out Yei Min's name, she ran out to greet him. But rather than the happy girl he hoped to see, she was distressed. Fear clouded her little face, and she'd lost weight.

She cried, "Everyone's yard is three times as big as it was before. Every family has fifteen wocs, fifteen gips, and at least eighteen ne-chicks in their coops."

Bai lifted Yei Min onto the sehor and urged the noble animal forward, growing ever closer to the village, which looked nothing like he remembered. The Land for All was crowded with gips and wocs. Ne-chicks were everywhere, perched on the roofs and sitting on door stoops, preening themselves in the sun and squabbling over territory.

When Bai's parents greeted him at the door of their cottage, he was shocked to see the change in them. They were fatter than their fattest gips.

He was happy to see them, and to meet his new twin

brothers, but after the greetings were over, he quickly turned his attention back to the village.

He asked, "What's happened here? The village is so different now."

"We're prospering, that's what," Bai's father said proudly as he toured his son around his family's greatly expanded property. "We eat all day and celebrate all night."

"But father, it's so crowded. Doesn't that worry you?"

Bai's father grinned and jovially patted Bai on the back.

"Worry? No, indeed. We're making great use of the Land for All now. No more wasted space."

Bai suspected that his father's perspective was flawed. If everyone kept expanding their farms, the Land for All might disappear one day. But he didn't push his point because he didn't want to dampen his homecoming celebration.

*At dinner, Bai's father sawed off
a healthy slice of gip...*

Bai's father laughed at his son's sour attitude. At dinner, he sawed off a healthy slice of gip to demonstrate the family's wealth, and plopped it onto Bai's plate.

Then the other children gathered around the table and dug into their own share of the food. Yei Min was the only child who picked at her food and left most of it untouched.

Bai tossed and turned all night, unsure what to do. Waking at dawn to the cock-a-doodle-doos of dozens of "serroots," he left his ducky sack and wandered through the village, deep in thought.

When he reached the well, he sat on the edge and contemplated his options. Should he confront his parents, or hold his tongue, waiting to see what would happened next? It was a pivotal moment, for his decision sealed the village's fate.

"They won't listen," he told himself, "so what's the point? Better to spend my vacation taking care of my sister."

Over the next couple of weeks, Bai nursed Yei Min back to health, taking her on long rides through the forest to distract her mind and give her some pleasure. They went mostly at night, as both Lunera and Ru were high in the sky and the moons-light was bright. It was a lovely time, but as the moons waned and disappeared over the dawn horizon, it was time for Bai to return to school.

As he trotted away from the village, he waved goodbye to Yei Min with a great deal of reluctance. She looked scared.

Back at school once more, Bai had a hard time concentrating. He didn't let his grades slip, but he was troubled, and the headmaster sensed it. As soon as the time was right, he granted Bai another leave, lending him an even faster sehor than before.

*Galloping across the plains,*
*Bai was worried about Yei Min...*

"Off you go," he said, slapping the sehor on the flanks. "Take care of whatever is bothering you at home."

Worried sick about Yei Min, and determined to make good speed, Bai traveled light. Galloping across the plains, he couldn't wait to see his sister. Would she be okay?

She wasn't. When he reached the village outskirts and let out a cheery greeting, his sister didn't run out to greet him. Instead, he found her propped against a tree outside the family home, too weak to walk.

The rest of Bai's family was lean and listless, too.

"The animals aren't doing well," his father grunted as he led Bai into the house. "They're starving. I don't understand it. Everyone is hungry now. Each family is down to two wocs, two gips, and two ne-chicks, and if we slaughter those we'll have no chance for future woc-itties, gipitties, and ne-chicklets. I can't offer you anything for dinner tonight but thin soup."

Bai looked around. The Land for All was almost gone and the remaining grass was shriveled and brown.

With a sinking feeling, he put Yei Min to bed. She was burning up with fever. He cooled her down with wet towels and tucked her into her ducky sack.

"You sleep," he told her. "I'm going to talk with our parents."

Bai confronted his father and mother in the kitchen.

"Don't you see what's happened?" he asked urgently. "The Land for All is all used up. We must abandon our properties and flee this village at once. The livestock are starving. If we wait, we'll starve too."

"Nonsense," Bai's mother replied. "The Land for All has always provided."

Bai's father added, "Yes, it has. There's no reason to think it will let us down. We'll just wait out this hard time. We're in a slump, that's all."

Just then, there was a wailing from down below, and Bai looked out the window. Mrs. Chung, all skin and bones, was running around in circles.

She wailed, "Our gips are dead. They took a drink

from the well and then keeled over. Oh, this is terrible. Our wocs will be next. There's something wrong with the water in the well!"

Bai's parents leapt to their feet and raced outside to check on their own livestock. As they did, their neighbors followed suit.

Soon the air was alive with howls of despair.

"All the gips are dead," the villagers yelled, as they spilled out of their barns, sharing the dreadful news with one another. "And our ne-chicks have joined them. Not a one of them is left!"

For hungry people, it was all too much, and they started blaming each other.

"*You* poisoned the well!" Mr. Chung cried out, pointing an accusing finger at Mrs. Hing.

"I most certainly didn't," she snapped in her defense. "Why would I hurt my own livestock? Tell me that. Someone else did it."

"Maybe it's Mil!" cried another villager. "He founded this village. Perhaps he is jealous of how this town has

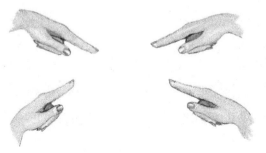

*The villagers blamed each other...*

grown, and wants to drive us away. He doesn't have the Land for All to himself anymore, does he, with those thirty-five children of his?"

With that, the starving people of Curimicu lost their senses and climbed over their neighbors' fences to steal their remaining wocs and dead gips and ne-chicks, and boil them up in pots of hot water.

Then the villagers' plight grew worse. The water they used for the boiling came from the same well that had poisoned their gips, and it made them horribly sick. The beautiful well, once flushed continuously by a lively spring, was almost empty, drained by overuse. And the slimy, muddy bottom was thick with "picnic grofs," now, that lived and bred in such conditions.

One by one, the villagers fell deathly ill, blaming one another as they clutched their bellies and wailed. Only the children escaped, following Bai into the safety of the forest, where they watched events unfold in shock and disbelief, their once lovely village in chaos.

"What happened?" the children asked each other. "Why are our parents fighting?"

Bai gathered them together to explain.

"They used up the Land for All, and now there's nothing left. They're scared for their lives and have lost their minds. We'll wait here until they come to their senses. Then we'll all move elsewhere. There's no place for us in Curimicu any longer, nor will there ever be again."

At that, Bai broke down in tears, regretting that he

hadn't spoken up the year before, when there was still time to avert the catastrophe.

"It's not enough to listen and watch," he told Yei Min, while she smoothed his long hair, adding her sorrow to his. "I'll do better in the future."

They hid out in the forest for two days, but soon hunger and thirst took their toll, and Bai led them back to the village and the sad sight that awaited them there.

The place was in ruins, and the adults were milling about, desperately searching for their children. They were a pathetic lot, so ashamed by their behavior that they avoided one another's eyes.

Bai quickly took over. The people were at loose ends, and needed a leader. He was the only one who seemed to know what to do, and the villagers quickly fell into line.

"Gather your belongings," he directed them. "We'll leave this very day. There's fertile land south of here where we can start again."

A few hours later, they were gone, leaving Curimicu in the grip of the grofs and their future in the hands of Bai, who was determined to enact a Rule of Law that protected the Land for All. In the end, he did just that, and the new village of Micuciru prospered sustainably, with five wocs and five gips per family, and ten ne-chicks apiece.

Bai returned to Curimicu only once after that, to finish a complete history of the place, which he carefully recorded on a scroll—the one I fortuitously found so many centuries later.

I'm grateful to Bai for completing the tale. Otherwise, I wouldn't know that the poison picnic grofs ate everything in Curimicu after the people left, feasting on what remained of the villagers' lifeless livestock. In a celebration of abundance, they recklessly reproduced in huge numbers, spawning millions of hungry picnic groflings, just as stupid and blind to the *danger of the Land for All* as the people of Curimicu had been.

When they'd eaten all the leftovers in the village, the grofs spread out as far as the mud would take them, crawling and hopping up river valleys and down ravines, gobbling up everything they could find.

Finally, just like the people of Curimicu, they ran out of what they needed to survive, and turned on each other. For when the Land for All is gone, it's every grof (or man) for himself, and the outcome is always the same.

# 4

# The Six Woes of Werd

*In which a trickster proves wise,*
*and a girl wins what she loves.*

Six centuries ago, forty-eight degrees in south latitude and thirty degrees in east longitude, twenty-four miles west of the village of Ixs, there once lived a man named Werd who had exactly six woes.

Six-woed Werd was a silk rancher by trade, the owner of a thriving colony of small-eyed-big-eyed cave "p-siders." They had two big eyes and twelve small eyes apiece, and most people thought they were the ugliest creatures on Urth. But their silk was highly prized because it was delicate to the touch yet strong as steel. Demand was always high, and Werd, who was a widower, was quite rich, living with his two children in a sprawling estate overlooking magnificent Half Moons Bay.

Despite appearances, though, Werd's world wasn't

all rosy. You see, he focused on his woes instead of his good fortune, and, like most people who do that, he was miserable, convinced he was the unluckiest man alive.

Werd's daughter, Laly, couldn't have been more different. She noticed every good thing and leapt from her bed each morning, eager to start the day. She loved the p-siders and gave them names like "Betty" and "Pearl." But Werd ignored her obvious interest in the valuable creatures, keen that his son, Dyna, should take over the business one day. In Werd's time, fathers passed their estates to their sons, not to their daughters, and he was a man of tradition.

Unfortunately, Dyna was terrified of the p-siders. Whenever Werd asked him to help with the colony, he fainted dead away. It was Werd's greatest woe, and he had no idea what to do about it.

One morning, he decided to begin writing down his woes, to keep better track of them.

"I'll make my list on the first day of every Lunera month," he vowed. "With Urth's two moons, I can choose Lunera months or Ru months. But Lunera months are shorter, and I have many woes."

Thus, when the first day of the Lunera month of Nuje arrived, Werd began his new routine.

*My toe is broke,*
*My "gip" is old,*
*My "sehor" threw three riders.*

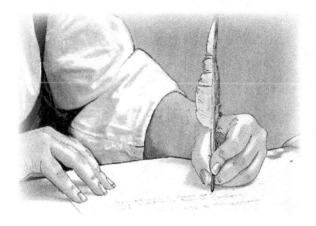

*Werd recorded his woes...*

*My barn has "tars,"*
*I'm much too fat,*
*But worst of all for a man like me,*
*My son is scared of p-siders.*

Gips, sehors, and tars were Urth animals, and back in Werd's day, they were common on farms. Most people had no trouble with them, but Werd (being who he was) found them an endless source of worry.

Nuje was a lovely time of year. The "head grass" was green and growing fast. The sky was impossibly blue, raked clean of clouds by the brisk, seasonal winds. But Werd noticed none of this beauty as he wheeled his cart down to Ixs that day, heavy with silk for the market. Instead, he stewed over his six woes as he hobbled along on his broken toe, feeling sorrier for himself than ever, now that his woes were on paper.

*The gossip sold milk and cheese...*

When he reached the busy town, he set up his stall, as was his habit, and laid out his fine silk. But before any customers showed up, the woman next to him, who was selling milk and cheese, shared some exciting gossip.

"A great sage has come to the region, and is staying tonight at Ixs Inn," she cried, her eyes alight. "His name is Tutsea and his reputation precedes him. He's known far and wide as a man who is always right. Apparently, he's never wrong. I'm going to ask him how to get my 'ne-chicks' to lay more eggs, as I'm only getting eight eggs per Ru month from the nine of them."

"A man who's always right. Never wrong?" Werd repeated to himself. "I want to meet this Tutsea fellow. Perhaps he can help me solve my woes, because, goodness knows, I have six and need help."

It was easy for Werd to get an audience with Tutsea, despite the man's celebrity. The sage was clever, and liked nothing more than to work for wealthy clients, who could pay him well for his services. He sized Werd up immediately and sensed he was an easy mark.

As Werd poured out his woes, Tutsea listened. Then he told the downcast man exactly what he wanted to hear.

"It may take a long time and cost you much to get rid of your woes. But if you do what I say for as long as it takes, one day you won't have any more woes. Guaranteed. I am always right. Never wrong. You'll see."

Werd was delighted and invited Tutsea to move in with him for the duration of their work together.

"I have plenty of room," Werd assured him, "and my daughter will be happy. She thinks I spend too much time worrying and will be thrilled that you've agreed to rid me of my six woes."

Tutsea smiled. Events were unfolding just as he'd hoped. He would enjoy living in Werd's fine house, eating his rich food for a while.

Laly greeted Tutsea warmly, excited that he'd come to cheer up her father. She was sick and tired of all his moping and hoped Tutsea had the power to put an end to it.

"I must have the grandest room in the house," Tutsea informed her, looking around with satisfaction. "I need an unobstructed view of the western horizon so I can see the moons-sets. I can't think well otherwise, and it's going to take much hard thinking to help your father."

Laly gladly agreed, giving him the family's living room, which was spacious and overlooked the ocean. She

*Werd's grand house looked out to sea...*

herself lived in a tiny room in the attic, where she kept nothing but her "ducky sack," a book, and a little lantern—a situation that suited her simple needs just fine.

True to his word, Tutsea began counselling his new benefactor the next morning. After a delicious breakfast of ne-chick eggs, crispy gip bacon, toast, and juice, Tutsea instructed, "Stay off your feet for one Lunera month. Let Dyna take the silk to market instead. Mark my words, Werd. Your toe will heal right up. I am always right. Never wrong. You'll see."

It was excellent advice. Although the cart lost a wheel when Dyna accidentally rolled it into a ditch, Werd's toe was back to normal by the end of Nuje, just as Tutsea had predicted.

No longer limping, Werd was well pleased. In fact, he

was so enamored with Tutsea that he didn't notice that he *still* had six woes on the first day of the Lunera month of Jylu. Crossing out the old woe, he penned in the new one:

> ~~My toe is broke~~ My cart is broke,
> My gip is old,
> My sehor threw three riders.
> My barn has tars,
> I'm much too fat,
> But worst of all for a man like me,
> My son is scared of p-siders.

As Werd made his way to the p-sider colony on that fine morning, the tall, healthy head grass rustled in the warm wind and whispered its abundance. But he was too absorbed with his woes to notice.

Laly, though, enjoyed the happy scene as she walked along.

*Laly marveled at the rich head grass...*

"Look at the rich, golden grain," she cried, in awe of its magnificence. "Surely, Jylu is the most wonderful month of the year. We have much to celebrate!"

When they reached the cave where the big-eyed-small-eyed p-siders lived, Laly went to work with a will.

"Patricia," she laughed. "You naughty girl. Come back here with that silk of yours. I need to gather it all, you know, so father can take it to market and come home with plenty of fat insects to feed you."

Laly took a seat on the ground, coaxing Patricia toward her, and when the p-sider sat down beside her, she tickled her spinnerets playfully.

Werd helped with the colony, but his thoughts were elsewhere, as they usually were. With so many woes, he had no time to lose. He was eager to get back to the house. Tutsea had offered to help him with his second woe that afternoon.

Back at home, Werd lunched with the sage. As Tutsea finished off a plate of "woc" ribs and fluffy biscuits slathered with butter, he pointed his fork at Werd and said:

"It's time to slaughter that aging gip of yours and buy a young, pregnant female. Mark my words, Werd. You'll have a sty full of gipitties before long. I am always right. Never wrong. You'll see."

Once more, Tutsea's counsel was sound, for although the lively new gipitties knocked over their water trough several times a day, and the hay in the sty got moldy, Werd had nothing but young gips now, and he was pleased.

In fact, he was so sure that Tutsea was guiding him well that he barely realized that he *still* had six woes on the first day of Ugusta, one Lunera month later:

*My cart is broke,*
~~*My gip is old*~~ *My sty has mold,*
*My sehor threw three riders.*
*My barn has tars,*
*I'm much too fat,*
*But worst of all for a man like me,*
*My son is scared of p-siders.*

Ugusta was the month of the head grass harvest, and Werd, Dyna, and the migrant workers labored hard to bring it in. Laly chipped in, too, eagerly breathing in the fragrant, freshly cut vegetation and enjoying the sweet singing of the nesting "rewns."

*The rewns sang sweetly...*

"Surely, this is the best time of the year," she exclaimed. "Just listen to the sights and the sounds in these fields. And the p-siders are laying lots of eggs. Come winter, we'll have twice as much silk as we did last year. We have much to celebrate!"

Werd rolled his eyes at Laly's enthusiasm. Didn't his clueless daughter realize how many woes they had? But when the great harvest was over and Tutsea approached

him about solving the matter with his sehor, Werd forgot all about Laly. He had lawsuits pending against him
in the courts. He'd hired three wocboys to break his
high-spirited sehor and it had bucked all three off its
back and into the hospital.

"Pay them off," Tutsea advised. "You have plenty of
golden tidbits in the bank. Those men will drop their
complaints when you fill their pockets with money. It's
the quickest, easiest way to handle your third woe. I am
always right. Never wrong. You'll see."

It was a sensible idea, and while the sehor bucked
off four more wocboys while Werd was settling the first
three lawsuits, at least he didn't have seven lawsuits on
his plate at the same time.

In fact, he was so hypnotized by Tutsea's apparent wisdom that he was only slightly annoyed when he
noticed that he *still* had six woes when he picked up his
pen on Tespember first:

> *My cart is broke,*
> *My sty has mold,*
> ~~*My sehor threw three riders*~~. *My sehor threw four riders,*
> *My barn has tars*
> *I'm much too fat,*
> *But worst of all for a man like me,*
> *My son is scared of p-siders.*

Tespember was always hot and dry as a bone, and
Werd couldn't wait for the sweltering days to pass.

But Laly saw wonder in it, because p-siders bred in Tespember. She busied herself happily, dreaming up new names for the p-siderlings as they emerged from their eggs, tiny and oh-so-cute.

Meanwhile, Tutsea advised Werd how to handle the woe in his barn.

"What are the tars eating?" he asked. "There must be something in the barn or they'd go elsewhere."

*The woe in Werd's barn...*

Sure enough, Werd found three sacks of grain with little teeth marks all over them.

"I can't believe I left these here," he berated himself. "What a stupid man I am. No wonder I have so many woes."

Werd hauled the sacks away and burned their ruined contents. And, sure enough, just as Tutsea had foretold, by the time Tocober rolled around, all the tars had disappeared. Werd was delighted.

What he failed to recognize, at least at first, was that tars ate nasty insects called leci, as well as grain. Soon, Dyna's hair was full of them.

While Dyna fussed and scratched, Laly focused on the rains, which had come at last. Tocober was the season when the storms swept in, and she loved to stand in the downpours with her arms thrown open to the sky and her fingers stretched out wide.

Leci were no laughing matter though, and, when Werd wrote out his list of woes for Vonember, his hand shook with anger.

> *My cart is broke,*
> *My hay has mold,*
> *My sehor threw four riders.*
> ~~*My barn has tars*~~ *My kid has leci,*
> *I'm much too fat,*
> *But worst of all for a man like me,*
> *My son is scared of p-siders.*

Tutsea noticed that Werd was unusually upset, and swooped in to distract him, promising to address his fifth woe in record time.

"Laly is an excellent cook," Tutsea pointed out. "She whips up rich desserts for the family every night. If you lay off them for a Lunera month or so, leaving them for the rest of us to eat, you'll slim down. I am always right. Never wrong. You'll see."

This new instruction didn't sit well with Werd, because he was fond of sweets. But with six woes, he couldn't be choosy, so he did as he was told.

The month crawled by, and Werd was more miserable than ever. In the evenings, he sat in the kitchen, staring at the cupboard like a hungry "tac," a domestic feline famous for its love of food. But he didn't cheat. Not once. And by the time Cedember swept in, with its freezing rain and snow, he was leaner than he'd been in decades.

He was pleased at first, and vain in front of mirrors. But when his shortest belt became too long, he realized he'd gone too far.

In his office, chilled to the quick because he had no fat on his bones, Werd was so discouraged that he almost gave up writing his woes. But it was a habit for him now, so he kept on going.

> *My cart is broke,*
> *My hay has mold,*
> *My sehor threw four riders.*
> *My kid has leci,*
> ~~*I'm much too fat*~~ *I'm much too lean,*
> *But worst of all for a man like me,*
> *My son is scared of p-siders.*

Just as he finished his list, Laly bounded up the stairs, thrilled to share the news that the p-siderlings had started spinning.

"They're all grown up," she said with pride. "Come down to the colony with me, father, and let me show you."

The contrast between his six-woed list and his daughter's glee was too much for Werd at that moment, and he snapped.

"You stay away from the p-sider colony!" he barked, coming halfway out of his chair. "I *forbid* you to go there anymore. It's time for Dyna to take over, and for *you* to find a husband."

Laly was devastated, but she didn't dare disobey her

*Laly wept over the p-siders...*

father. Instead, she fled to her room and wept.

Meanwhile, a hopping mad Werd marched down to the kitchen, where Tutsea was eating a generous slice of Laly's bluffberry pie.

"I still have six woes!" he screamed, throwing his list into the sage's copious lap. "Just look. Each time you helped me solve one, another popped up to take its place. I'm no better off than the day you came to town. Yet, you *swore* you'd rid me of my woes. I want answers, man, or I'll throw you from this house and ruin your reputation!"

Tutsea rose to his feet, tossing his napkin to one side. He was a tall, imposing man, and Werd immediately felt less certain of his position.

"Surely you want to solve your *sixth* woe," Tutsea intoned. "It's your worst one, is it not? Would you really want me to leave this house before that issue was resolved?"

Werd was beyond words at that point. Intimidated, he simply stared, waiting for Tutsea's counsel.

"Break with tradition and split your estate, Werd. Go to your lawyer and change your will. Pass the colony along to Laly, who loves the p-siders and will tend them well."

Werd's skin, like those of all Urth people, was lavender in hue. Now it flushed maroon.

"Don't be ridiculous," he said hoarsely, finding a smidgeon of his voice again. "Estates are passed, intact, from fathers to sons. Daughters marry and leave home. Everyone knows that."

"No law makes it so," Tutsea replied. "It's just a tradition. Wake up, man. Listen to your daughter weeping in her little attic room. She's crying her heart out over those ugly p-siders. That's love, Werd. *Pure love.* Giving her the colony is the only way to vanquish your sixth woe. Your *only* way."

Werd broke down in tears. He recognized the truth in Tutsea's words. Laly's fierce love was no match for his ties to convention. Love, he realized, was the most powerful force on Urth.

The next day, Werd signed the papers, deeding the colony to Laly and the fertile land to Dyna. Tutsea had vanquished his worst woe at last, and he

*Werd deeded the p-siders to Laly and the fertile land to Dyna...*

had to admit that with only five woes left to solve, his heart was a bit lighter.

His relief (of course) didn't last long. Another woe was just around the corner, and turned out to be his worst ever. On his way back home, in a blinding storm, he was struck by lightning. A few hours later, a passing wocboy (riding Werd's now-tame sehor) found him on the road and rushed him to a doctor, but it was too late. Poor Werd, once again six-woed, died that evening.

The whole town buzzed with the news, and many people were outraged. Tutsea had promised to rid Werd of his woes, and now look at the poor man. Dead as a poisoned tar!

They came in droves to Werd's funeral, and when Tutsea rose to say a few words, they attacked him with their ripe fury.

"You promised this man he'd have no more woes!" they cried angrily, closing in. "You lied. You lived in Werd's fine house. You ate his rich food for many Lunera months. Yet as soon as you helped him eliminate one woe, he got another! *And that's how life is, isn't it?* Everyone has woes. You knew this universal truth all along, and tricked Werd into thinking otherwise."

Tutsea raised his hand to quiet the crowd. He had something important to say, that he hoped would calm them down. His golden reputation depended on them listening, so he spoke up loud and clear, for all to hear:

"I am always right. Never wrong. The man who lies in this coffin started out with six woes and now he has none. Woes plague only the living. It's not possible to have woes when you're dead."

There was a short silence as the villagers stared at Tutsea. All of them could see the truth in his words, plain as day. Dead men didn't have woes. How could they?

A disgruntled murmur swept through the crowd. In various ways, they said the same thing. "Tutsea's right! Problems belong to the living. He may have tricked our friend and taken advantage of his ignorance, but he wasn't wrong about poor Werd's woes."

Tutsea smiled, pleased that the villagers had changed their minds so quickly. He'd visited many towns in his time, ridding people of woes, and he'd found that angry mobs weren't always so easy to convince.

"You're wise people," he praised them. "I wish I could stay among you. But I must be off, for I have another job waiting for me."

Then, without further ado, he left Ixs forever, his status intact, off to the town of Neves, where a rich man with seven woes needed his help.

The next morning, Laly sat down at her father's desk and gazed out the window. Although the fields were knee-deep in snow and the wind's breath was icy, she saw only

loveliness in the stark landscape. There was such simplic-
ity and beauty in the season. One colorful male rewn that
hadn't flown south with the others pecked at the seed in
the bird feeder with unabashed pleasure.

"No more bemoaning woes, father," she whispered,
planting a kiss on his portrait, which she held so dear.
"There's no end to them in this life. Better to notice what's
right, and be happy. There's always much to celebrate."

She crumpled his list of woes and tossed it in the
trash. Then she withdrew a fresh piece of paper from a
drawer, picked up her father's pen and wrote:

> *The cart works fine,*
> *The hay is dry,*
> *Our sehor has nine riders,*
> *The leci are dead,*
> *We're all well-fed,*
> *But best of all for a girl like me...*
>
> *I got the p-siders.*

# 5

# THE RULE OF E

*In which a maiden uses her wits*
*to escape a wicked grandfather*

vil in the world takes many guises, and in E's case it came in the form of her grandfather. He was a bent and crotchety man, who might have been pitied had he not been so diabolical. But everyone in Daventry Village, where they lived, knew his true nature and felt sorry for E. She was an orphan of sorts. Her parents had died the day she was born, brought down by a mysterious ailment that her grandfather refused to explain. She had no siblings, and, despite her striking beauty, no one to love her but a boy in the village, who was forced to keep his distance, and an ugly, blind "g'do" (guh-doo) named Swie.

G'dos were much like dogs, and, though elderly Swie was "eyes-less," he knew much, for he had an astounding

*E had no one to love her but a blind g'do named Swie...*

nose. He could smell wickedness and knew exactly what kind of man E's grandfather was. And, because in the olden times, g-dos could talk to the ones they love, he tried his best to give E good advice and slept at the end of her "ducky sack" each night, in camaraderie.

"Sweep the hearth and gather the eggs from the 'ne-chick' coops, you silly, lazy girl!" E's grandfather bellowed one morning. It was the usual kind of dawn greeting E received from him. "Then chop the wood and make a fire to keep my toes warm. And hurry. I'll not have you keep me waiting."

E was no push-around. She was a spritely young woman, with a mind of her own. She knew that other girls in the village weren't treated so cruelly. As often happened, she didn't keep her tongue.

"You work me too hard, Grandfather. I don't have the strength for chopping wood. None of my friends are forced to do this kind of labor. You should hire a strapping young man with muscles."

"You are a disobedient, arrogant girl!" her grandfather retorted, coming after her with his cane. "You have no power in this house."

E reached for a poker from the fireside, prepared to fight him off, but Swie intervened.

"Bide your time," he urged, as he did when his mistress lost her temper. He knew if she didn't remain calm, she would be harshly punished. "One day you will find a way out of your terrible situation, but only if you use your wits, not your anger."

All E's grandfather heard was "BARK! BARK! BARK!" because Swie didn't love him. But E heard the words, and took her companion's counsel, though it was difficult to swallow.

"Oh, Swie," she said when they got to the ne-chick coop, "I *hate* grandfather so. How will I ever get out from under his thumb? All of my friends have 'renamed' themselves, and left me behind."

It was true. Her friend Amy had scrambled around the letters in her birth name, as Urth's young people are required to do when renaming themselves. Then she'd left her parents' home, as May, to go to university. Anna, now known as Nana, was a dancer in a famous company that toured the country, far and wide. But with a one letter name, poor E couldn't follow suit. While her friends moved on with their lives, becoming adults who could make their own decisions, E was forever destined to be a child, though her maturing body suggested otherwise.

Swie replied, "I'm well aware of what your grandfather did. I saw it all when I still had my puppy eyes. When he lifted you from your cradle, he laughed and laughed, even though his own son and daughter-in-law had just lost their lives. And he said aloud:

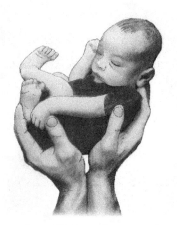

*I will name her E. Just one letter. That way, she can never rename herself and she won't be able to leave me. She'll live in my house until I die, doing whatever I say. An unrenamed child must obey her elders. It is the law of the land. Oh! I am brilliant. I'm surprised no one has thought of this trick before!*

*"I will name her E…"*

E knew the story all too well. Swie had told it to her many times. Still, hearing it always made her feel better, knowing that Swie knew the truth first-hand, and was on her side.

E gathered the eggs resentfully, and when she chopped the wood, she complained bitterly.

"Look at that," she cried, when the axe failed to meet its mark and nearly sliced off her left foot. "If I keep this up I'll be lame for life!"

There wasn't much wood that evening, and her grandfather berated her. It was the usual kind of dusk greeting she got from him, no matter

*E almost lost her foot to the axe…*

how hard she'd labored.

"Stupid, incompetent girl," he accused. "Lying about all day, dreaming romantic dreams, no doubt. Neglecting the axe."

"I can have whatever dreams I like," E cried, her face burning. "And I didn't play around. I worked so hard that I nearly hurt myself!"

"Hold back!" Swie implored her, running up and laying down at her feet. "Your grandfather's greatest fear is that you'll leave him and he'll have to take care of himself. That's why he doesn't want you daydreaming about love. But one day you will find a way out of your terrible situation—*if* you use your wits, not your anger."

"BARK! BARK!" was what Grandfather heard, and he ignored the ugly g'do who was eyes-less, and therefore (in his mind), useless. Had he known that Swie was encouraging E to find a way to be free, he would have thrown him into the street and been done with him. But as it was, he found E a lot easier to control when Swie was around.

E respected Swie and kept her mouth shut for the rest of the evening as she served her grandfather dinner, just the way he liked it, and cleaned up afterwards.

When she crawled into her ducky sack, her muscles cramping with exhaustion and her mind swirling in rage, Swie did his best to comfort her by climbing onto her tummy and licking her fingers.

"What am I to do?" E asked in exasperation. "I'm

*Yaj declared his love with a bouquet of wildflowers...*

nearly a woman now, and I have eyes for a boy in the village who is handsome, clever, and kind. He loves me. He finally declared it yesterday, kneeling before me with a bouquet of wild-flowers when I was out working in the fields. His name is Yaj and, when I see him, my belly flutters. He has a wonderful sense of humor and makes me laugh, despite my despair here at home. If I were free, I'd run off with him in a heartbeat."

"I'm well aware of your feelings for him," Swie told her sympathetically. "When the two of you are together, the delightful perfume of your love fills the air. My nose tells me much, and I can smell when two people are meant to be together. I wish the laws of the land permitted him to court you properly. As it is, he must be very careful and never let on what he feels."

"I wish I could tell him that I love him, too," E fumed, her eyes filling with hot tears. "But I simply *can't*. It wouldn't be fair to encourage him. A girl like me, with a single letter name, can't grow up and become a wife, or anything else she chooses to be."

"That's true enough," replied Swie. "But stay calm. One day you will find a way out of your terrible situation, but only if you use your wits, not your anger."

That night, after E and Swie had retired to bed, there was a knock on the cottage door, and E's grandfather, who was still awake, answered it. To his astonishment, a man of royal birth stood before him with an important offer that took him completely off guard. He was Prince Jardon and explained that he'd seen E the day before, out in the fields, as he was riding past. Never had he seen a more beautiful creature, and he was determined to have her for his very own.

E's grandfather bowed and groveled, but at the same time struck a shrewd deal. He'd give up his granddaughter, but the prince must allow him to live at the castle, in luxury, where he'd be waited on, hand and foot, the rest of his days.

Prince Jardon agreed. The grandfather of his new wife could expect no less.

The next morning, E rose from her ducky sack as exasperated as ever with her lot in life, and made her way to the kitchen to start the fire and make her grandfather his tea.

But, instead of his usual sour greeting, her grandfather smiled at her. It was a hideous attempt; his mouth smiled but his eyes didn't. He looked like an evil clown, and E didn't trust his apparent change in attitude one whit.

Likewise, Swie smelled the fact that the old man was being two-faced, and the clever g'do remained on his guard.

"E, my dear," her grandfather wheedled in a toady-ing voice, "I have been *much* too harsh with you these many years. I can see that now. It's as clear as day and as dark as a moons-less night. Come and sit by the fire while I make your breakfast."

E balked.

"Make my breakfast?" she asked sarcastically. "After all these years, you're going to wait on *me* for a change? How absurd. A wicked man doesn't turn good overnight!"

Her grandfather rose to his full height and seemed ready to strike her (as he would have done to counter an outburst like that in the past), but he caught himself just in time.

"Indeed, I deserve all your hatred," he admitted, sinking to his knees before her. "I have been a terrible grandfather to you. But it's time to heal all that."

He didn't wait for a reply. Instead, he knee-walked over to the hearth and got busy preparing E a cup of tea.

E frowned, and called Swie over to her.

"What do you smell?" she asked under her breath. "Is he sincere?"

"No," Swie replied. "He stinks to high heaven. Some-

*To E's surprise, her grandfather prepared the tea...*

thing has caused this sudden transformation, though I don't yet know what it is. I advise you to keep your head. Play along. This *may* be the day you find a way out of your terrible situation, but only if you use your wits, not your anger."

After serving E her tea, her grandfather turned his attention to breakfast. He burned everything, including his fingers, as he hadn't cooked in many years. But E pretended to enjoy the meal, and ate each charred and bitter bite, all the time petting Swie's back to draw strength from his resolve.

"The bacon is so crisp," she said. "And the ne-chick eggs so perfectly fried. I can see—as clear as day and as dark as a moons-less night—that I was wrong about you. You are a wonderful, caring grandfather, and I'm happy that you and I can finally set things right between us."

E's grandfather patted her on the head, an act of false endearment that made her squirm. Then he set to work washing and drying the dishes, breaking one or two in the process, and slicing open his right thumb.

Still, he didn't utter a word of complaint.

"I'm so confused, Swie," E had to admit. "What game do you think he's playing?"

Neither of them knew, but Swie, once again, urged patience.

"It *is* rather funny seeing him like this, is it not?" he asked. "Bustling about the kitchen, creating chaos."

E agreed. It certainly made her feel a bit better to be waited on for once, especially by *him!*

E and Swie watched in wonder as the once-abusive man stripped the beds and did the laundry, ripping several sheets along the way. In the end, the linens were still dirty, and when he hung them out to dry, he lost two ducky sack covers to the wind.

A little before noon, Swie became thoughtful. Sitting up, he took several deep sniffs, his black nose wiggling.

"What is it, Swie?" E asked, watching him closely. "What do you smell?"

"Strange. It is a foul odor, and unfamiliar to me," he replied. "A party of visitors is coming to our cottage. It will be here soon."

Swie was right. About half an hour later, there was a great flurry of activity outside, and E rushed to the window to see an amazing sight. A carriage embossed with gold glinted in the sunlight, with no less than six handsome white "sehors" at the lead, tossing their heads with pent-up energy and looking magnificent.

"What is this?" E asked Swie, whose nose was still on high alert. "A golden carriage? Why, it must be Prince Jardon. There's no other explanation."

At that moment, E happened to look across the street, beyond the fine carriage, and saw Yaj standing in the fields, looking directly at her. His beautiful eyes—the ones framed by long brown lashes—seemed unmoved by the golden carriage and its fancy occupants. His attention was all on her. It seemed to E that for one heavenly moment they were alone in the Universe together, just the two of them, and her heart soared.

But it was no use. The idea of love with Yaj was hopeless, so she tore her eyes away from his, returning her focus to the spectacle of the carriage once more.

Prince Jardon was known,

*Yaj looked directly at E*

far and wide, as the only member of the royal family who ever left the palace. He was the fourteenth of fourteen male heirs, so his chance of ever becoming a king was remote. Instead, his job was to collect taxes from the people and throw his weight around to remind them who was boss. He loved to make new laws, and was known to do so at a whim, whenever it served his purpose.

"I believe you're right. It's Prince Jardon," Swie replied in astonishment. "I can smell the smugness that he's famous for."

E watched in disbelief as the prince emerged from the carriage, a manservant holding the door for him and laying out a purple carpet. The prince was a fat man, near middle age, with a pompous air about him, and E disliked him immediately.

*Prince Jardon had a*
*pompous air about him...*

"I thought princes were young and handsome like Yaj," she whispered to Swie. "But this man is more like my grandfather than the princes in my imagination."

Swie agreed, his nose wrinkled in disgust.

Prince Jardon stalked up the path to their front door, and E's grandfather, who'd also seen him coming, rushed to let him in.

"You have a g'do," Prince Jardon commented with disdain as E's grandfather greeted him in the traditional way for male subjects, bowing before him until his head was only a few inches from the ground. "His barking hurts my royal ears."

"Yes, your Majesty, we do have a g'do in this house. But it's not *my* g-do. It's the faithful companion of your future wife, my granddaughter. She is quite enchanted with him, I can assure you, though I've never quite figured out why. He is eyes-less and dumb as a stone."

This time, Swie got angry, but E placed a firm hand on his agitated back. As unnerved as she was that the prince wanted her to be his wife, she sensed the need for caution.

"Hush, Swie," she whispered urgently. "We must both keep our heads. Stay calm."

"Imagine that," Swie thought, no longer angry. "We've switched roles. My mistress is the counselor now, and I'm the one who needs instruction. Oh, she has learned well!"

When Prince Jardon entered the cottage and saw E standing with Swie, he beamed with pleasure.

She curtseyed respectfully, as was the expectation for a young woman, and tried to look happy and honored to meet him.

"I was riding by this cottage yesterday," he told her by way of explanation, "and I saw you standing in a field, holding a bouquet of wildflowers. You are, by far, the most beautiful maiden I have ever laid eyes on, and I've decided to take you as my own."

E was about to cry out that she'd never let him *own* her. Why would she leave one form of slavery for another? But she didn't utter a peep.

"I need to keep a cool head so anger doesn't cloud my thinking. I'll bet Grandfather knew all about the prince's infatuation and plans to use it to his advantage." (She was right, of course.)

"Well," continued the prince when E failed to respond. "I suppose you'd like a say in the matter, young lady. Speak up and tell me you accept my proposal, so we can be wed today."

E opened her mouth to explain her situation. As an unrenamed person she couldn't marry him (even if she'd wanted to, which she didn't). But suddenly, out of nowhere, she had an idea.

E thought to herself, "I will plant the notion that he can make a *new* rule regarding my name, allowing me to rename myself so he can take me as his bride. He can't alter the old Renaming Rules. They are written in stone from the dawn of time. But he *does* have the power to dream up clever ways around the law. He's famous for that." She was sure he'd come up with a solution to meet his end.

"Oh, fine Sir," E cried, using her reason to its full effect, mirroring the wisdom of Swie. "I can't believe you admire a village girl like me. I'm duly humbled and flattered. You are most kind."

Prince Jardon was pleased. He took E's reply as a "yes" to his marriage proposal. The day was going just as he'd expected.

"Then I will have my servants make arrangements straight away, and the sooner the better, for I'm not a patient man, nor do I need to be."

"I'm so sorry your Majesty," E replied, her face a mask of distress. "But you're too quick. I can't leave my grandfather's home and become your wife in the palace. I haven't renamed myself, and the Renaming Rules prohibit a girl like me from doing so."

"What's that?" Prince Jardon boomed. "A young lady your age who hasn't renamed herself? That's odd, odd, indeed. Why not?"

"My name is E," she explained, "a name with one letter only. So you see, I can't scramble the letters in my name to create a rename in the usual way. I'm quite stuck."

The prince was displeased, and turned savagely on E's grandfather.

"What is this atrocity?" he barked. "A girl with the name of E? That's ridiculous! Who caused this to happen? I must punish him immediately!"

E's grandfather hung his head.

"It's my fault," he admitted as the fat prince glared at him with disapproval. "But you must understand. I lost my son and dear daughter-in-law on the very day that this lovely child was born. I was terribly distraught and made a foolish decision. In my anguish, I named her E, so I could keep her safe in my care all her life. I was so worried about her, being an orphan and all."

Inwardly, Swie scoffed, and might have rolled his eyes if he'd had any. He was glad, for once, that he was blind. His eye-rolling might have interfered with the plan that E was cleverly hatching. The odor coming off her body was one of excitement, not disgust, at her grandfather's outrageous falsehoods. She was onto something, and Swie couldn't wait to find out what it was.

"So you see," E said, "our love is quite impossible." Then she continued craftily, "Someone very powerful would need to create a *new* rule that rescued children like me, so they could rename themselves and make their own decisions. But what sort of person has that kind of authority? I'm sure there's no one like that."

The prince could see the situation quite clearly now, and immediately arrived at a solution. He was a haughty man, but a clever one, and he decisively called for his scribe.

The man appeared at his side instantly, a pen at the ready.

"My dear," the prince said, turning back to E, "you

are in the presence of royalty. I can make new rules whenever I please, and they become the law of the land. I can't change the old Renaming Rules; we must all live by them. But through a masterful trick on my part, I can set you free."

The prince's chest puffed out in self-importance, and he raised his voice to signal to his scribe that his dictation had begun.

"There is a *new* rule," he decreed. *"The Rule of E.* From this day forward it is the law of the land. Children with the name of E can flip their single letter sidewise and choose the rename M."

$$\mathsf{E} \longrightarrow \mathsf{m}$$

The scribe took down every word of the prince's decree, and then Prince Jardon signed the proclamation with a flourish, delighted that he had dismissed the only obstacle to having E for his own.

"Oh, your Majesty!" E beamed, gazing at him like she was an infatuated girl who couldn't wait to accompany him to the palace to cater to his every whim. "I gratefully choose the rename M and thank you so much. Now I can be married."

*With a flourish, Prince Jardon claimed M for his own...*

"Then let it be so!" cried the prince. "Today, we'll begin our life together, you and I. It is all settled."

M glanced at Swie, who was smiling in the way that g'dos tend to do, his tongue hanging out. He smelled the delicious aroma of M's near-victory, and he couldn't help but drool.

"I can't *believe* I finally have a rename," M smiled, truly happy, but not in the way Prince Jardon assumed. "I am M now, and can make my own decisions at last. I owe this good fortune all to *you*."

Prince Jardon smiled, too, in the smug way that self-important rulers do, for his mission was complete.

Or so he thought.

"And now I have a Renaming Wish," M continued, blushing like a young maiden in love (which she was). "Let me declare it now and finish what we have started. All newly renamed children are permitted one, are they not?"

"Yes, indeed," he agreed. "It is the law of the land. No one, not even I, can deny you that, nor would I want to. As soon as I hear it, I'll make sure it's carried out straight away."

M paused for a few seconds, enjoying her rare moment of power after so many years of servitude.

Swie, meanwhile, started to laugh.

"HUFF! HUFF! HUFF!" was all that M's grandfather and the prince heard, but M understood, and it was all she could do to keep her own composure. The situation was quite hilarious, and she knew that she and Swie would chuckle about it for years.

The prince expected M to ask for "a wedding dress with white lace and pearls" (or some such request), but that's not what came out of her mouth.

Instead, she confidently said, "Well then, my Renaming Wish is to marry a local boy named Yaj. You see, I am quite in love with *him*, and he would never try to *own* me."

There was a brief silence while her words sunk in, and then her grandfather cried:

"You can't do that. You ungrateful child!"

But, of course, she could, and he knew it. And when M married Yaj, there'd be no palace and no one to do his bidding.

The prince was similarly incredulous as he help-lessly watched M slip from his near-grasp.

"My dear," he muttered, taking a step toward her, "surely you jest."

But M paid no attention. She'd already turned away, her thoughts so focused on Yaj that all she could muster was a simple "good-bye."

And with that, she gathered her things together and left her grandfather's house forever, Swie trailing behind her, proud of his mistress and delighted that she'd used her wits to free herself, for anger wouldn't have worked.

# 6

# The Astrovisionary's Apprentice

*In which a prince exposes a clever trickster and wins a crown.*

This story about a wicked man, a prince, and a king isn't as old as the sun, moons, and stars. However, it *is* as old as the hills, because it took place when Urth still had hills (and mountains, too) and people who lived among them.

On one such hill, in a bustling village on the banks of a wide salt lake, there lived a trickster named Rune Oft, who called himself an astrovisionary.

"Astrovisionary" is a mouthful, to be sure, and many people, unable to remember the unusual word, called him an astrologer (or whatever) behind his back. He used the stars to make predictions, which is what astrologers do, after all. But whenever Rune overheard them, he set the straight record crooked.

"Astrologers and other quacks tell you what *might* happen. But astrovisionaries, like me, tell you what *will*. And who would choose doubt over certainty? No one, that's who."

In truth, Rune was the quackiest of quacks, the adult version of the dishonest, all-too-clever boy he'd once been. Nevertheless, the villagers put their faith in him. You see, in the handy little universe he offered them, the future was a "done deal" written in the stars. No difficult choices were necessary. No outcome was anyone's fault. And being rather simple people, they bit the bait and dropped their hard-earned golden "tidbits" into Rune's outstretched palm, clinging to his predictions like little children.

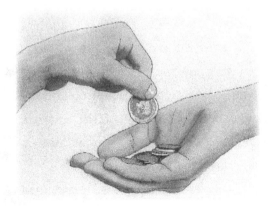

*The people dropped their hard-earned tidbits into Rune's hand...*

Thus, while Rune started life with nothing but a corrupt spirit and a crafty mind, he soon became famous. In fact, his reputation spread so far and wide that King Nad heard of him and sent his son, Prince Rich Satin, to serve as his apprentice.

"Find this astro-man (or whatever), and see if he can do as he says," the king directed him. "A man who can predict the future is worth a sea of diamonds to me, and I will hire him as my counselor."

Years before, Rich's mother, the queen, had tripped on the palace stairs and fallen to her death. "If only I'd known," King Nad often lamented. "If only I'd known, I could have been at the bottom of the stairs to catch her."

The tragedy had taken place when Rich was an infant, so he didn't feel the bitter loss, but his father had never gotten over it.

"If Rune can predict the future," Rich reasoned, "my father will never have to suffer a loss like that again, as he'll be warned in advance. I will seek out the astro-predictor (or whatever) and dispatch my mission well."

Prince Rich Satin was eager to go. As the eldest son of a king, he knew he had to prove himself or lose the crown to his younger brother. So he set off the next morning with a will, crossing many hills (and mountains, too) before arriving two days later at Rune's village.

When he reached the outskirts, he met an old woman on the road.

"Good evening, Grandmother," he cried, using the

*Prince Rich Satin crossed many*
*hills and mountains...*

traditional greeting for a woman her age. "Can you tell me where I can find the astro-promiser (or whatever)? I've come to serve as his apprentice."

"Rune lives up there," she replied, pointing up a crooked road that wound up a hill to a purple house capped with an observatory. "But he won't want an assistant. His art is a solitary one. He keeps his own company."

Rich Satin shrugged off the woman's warning. Having come far, and on an important mission, he was determined to meet the man who might shield his father from future pain.

"I'll climb the crooked road and tell Rune who I am," he thought. "He won't dare refuse the son of a king."

Prince Rich Satin was right. Although Rune nearly slammed the door in his face at first, worried that an apprentice might expose his trickery, his crooked little heart changed its greedy little tune when he learned that Rich Satin was a prince and in line to inherit the throne.

"You're King Nad's son?" Rune gasped. "Well, that changes *everything*. Naturally, I will be happy to take you under my wing. But beware, once you cross the threshold into this house, you'll be an apprentice, like any other, and must do what I say."

Rune's wicked mind was running in circles. The king had clearly sent Prince Rich to check him out, to see if he was truly capable of knowing, for certain, the future.

"It's worrisome," Rune thought. "But if I play my cards right, I can leave this village of fools and move to a *palace* of fools. And who would live in a village when he could live in a palace? No one, that's who."

It would involve an inconvenient change to his routine. The villagers believed that he consulted the heavens all night when, in point of fact, he slept, like everybody else, never setting foot in his grand observatory. He had a magnificent telescope and more than a dozen fancy, impressive-looking instruments up there, but they were all for show. He had no idea how to operate any of them.

"I'll work the boy hard and deprive him of sleep. He'll be too exhausted to notice that I'm a fraud. In less than one Ru month, I'll have him convinced that I'm the finest astrovisionary of all time."

To assert his dominance immediately, Rune assigned Rich a tiny room in the basement. Then he tossed him an apple and a little lantern.

*Rune threw Rich an apple and lantern...*

"Thank you," Rich said humbly. "I will learn much from an astro-master (or whatever) like you, and I am most grateful."

***"Astrovisionary!"*** Rune snapped, unable to hide his annoyance. He was sick and tired of people mucking up his title. "Now go to sleep. It will be the last good rest you'll get for a while."

An hour before dawn, Rune descended the stairs to the basement and rudely shook Rich awake.

"Milk the 'wocs,' gather the 'ne-chick' eggs, and cook our breakfast," he demanded, in a no-nonsense tone. "There is much to do for an apprentice like you, who must do his master's bidding."

Wocs were much like cows, and ne-chicks were similar to chickens. The palace kept many, and Rich was quite familiar with them. Being a prince, though, he wasn't used to tending them. Still, he accepted the fact that he was an apprentice in Rune's house, not a prince, and he headed to the yard.

Meanwhile, Rune put his feet up and watched the sunrise, pleased that he no longer had to milk the wocs, gather the ne-chick eggs, or cook breakfast for himself.

It was dark and chilly that morning, but Rich took to his work with a will. The cold, salty wind and the bright "cock-a-doodle-dos" of the "serroots" woke him right up. His chores in the barn and the coop took only an hour, and he was soon flipping ne-chick eggs over the stove. He'd watched the cooks at the palace do it, and, being a curious, helpful person by nature, he'd learned his way around the kitchen.

The breakfast, though simple, was hearty and tasty, and Rune was pleased.

"Who knew a prince could cook?" he thought. "I'll get more hard work out of him yet, the little sucker."

Rich excused himself to clean the dishes and then reappeared, wondering what would come next.

"I speak with the villagers precisely at nine," Rune told him, and, sure enough, at the appointed hour, the wicked man opened the door of his purple house for business.

Rich was astonished to see how many villagers were waiting for Rune's appearance. The line of men, women, and children wound all the way down the crooked road to the bottom of the hill.

"It's like this every day," Rune boasted. "The villagers depend on me. They'll come to me with their questions this morning, I'll consult the heavens tonight, and then I'll deliver the news, good or bad, tomorrow. They can't live without my services."

"But how on urth do you serve them all?" Rich Satin asked. "Surely, you can't read all their fortunes in a single night."

"Quite right," Rune replied. "I choose one lucky soul each day and send the rest away. As you'll see this evening, when we go to the observatory, astrovisioning is a high art and takes many hours."

The first person in line was an old man leaning on a cane, waiting for an answer from Rune. The day before, Rune had selected him as the "lucky soul." Unfortunately, it turned out that the man wasn't so lucky after all.

"Stop watering your fields. Your crops are doomed to fail this year, so what's the point? Such it was, is, and ever shall be. The heavens never lie. *No go home and do what you must.*"

The disappointed man departed, and Rune turned his attention to the other villagers.

One-by-one, they approached Rune. They were permitted to ask one question, and one question only.

"When will the rains come?" asked the first.

"Is my unborn child a boy or a girl?" asked the second.

"Where will I find my lost goose?" asked the third.

Rune scoffed at them all. "Those are *silly* inquiries," he said, as if they were naughty toddlers. "Not worth the time of a fine astrovisionary like me. Be off with you!"

But when the twenty-first man stepped forward, Rune's ears perked up.

"My son is the top student in his class," Red Barn explained. "He wants to go to the university. Tell me, will he pass the entrance exam in two weeks' time? If not, I need him in the fields to bring in the harvest. We're short staffed as it is."

"Finally, a *worthy* question," Rune praised his client, who beamed, in turn, with pleasure. "I will consult Rinor tonight. That great constellation controls such matters. When you come back tomorrow, I'll have your answer."

Red Barn thanked Rune and left in high spirits. After months of asking "silly" questions, he'd finally gotten one right. As he walked down the crooked road that wound down the hill, he tipped his hat merrily to his not-so-lucky neighbors. How fortunate he was!

*Red Barn left in high spirits...*

The selection process over, Rune dismissed the remaining villagers and ordered Rich to weed his overgrown garden.

"There is much to do for an apprentice like you," he reminded him, "who must do what I say."

Rich had never pulled weeds, but he'd watched the palace gardeners do it, and set to work, enjoying the fresh outdoors despite the labor.

Meanwhile, Rune whiled away the time snoozing on his veranda, pleased he no longer had to weed the garden himself.

Come evening, Rich cooked dinner and cleaned up. Then Rune donned a pair of impressive-looking spectacles, a tattered purple robe, and a crooked purple hat decorated with gold stars.

"We're in a trilogy," he informed Rich as he led him up to the observatory. "Both of Urth's moons are new and won't be in the sky tonight. It's the perfect moons-pattern for my work. We'll be able to see the stars without any interference."

Rich was susceptible to being manipulated by Rune. He'd failed "moons-studies" twice, under two different tutors. So, when Rune fiddled with the mighty telescope, spinning its intricate dials to create the illusion of intimate familiarity with the lenses, Rich had no clue he was faking.

"The eyepiece is in retrograde motion," Rune intoned, though he had no idea what "retrograde motion" meant. "I'll fix it later. Fortunately, we don't need the telescope tonight. Rinor reveals its secrets with the astrocalculator."

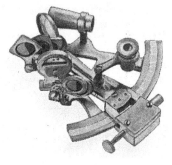

*Rune's astrocalculator was a silver instrument with many gears...*

Rune opened a small drawer in an ancient wooden desk inlaid with strange figures and pulled out a hand-sized silver instrument boasting dozens of tiny gears.

"I will use it to make the precise measurements I need for my compound calculations," he explained, with a look of grand superiority.

"*Retrograde motion, astrocalculator, precise,* and *compound,*" he snickered to himself. "Those fancy words will snow Rich under."

Rune aimed the astrocalculator at Rinor and spun the gears this way and that, pretending to measure its seventeen stars from every possible angle.

"Now that I have the apparent magnanimous of each star," he lied, "I can calculate the intelligence denominator of Red Barn's son."

Rich watched as Rune scribbled a series of equations in an otherwise empty notebook, peppering the pages with unfamiliar symbols that looked complex, indeed.

"This astro-astronomer (or whatever) certainly seems

to know what he's doing," Rich thought. "If this keeps up, I'll have a favorable report to give to my father."

Finally, around midnight, with a flourish of his pen, Rune circled the number seventy-one and pronounced his finding.

"Red Barn's boy is an idiot," he declared. "He has no chance of passing the entrance exam."

Rich felt sorry for Red Barn and his son, but didn't linger on his feelings for long. It was late and he was tired

*Rune circled the number 71 and pronounced his finding...*

from the day's difficult labor. All he wanted to do was to crawl into his "ducky sack" for some shut-eye.

But Rune had other plans for him.

"No sleep for you," his master barked, weighing him down with a thick tome called *The Sun, Moons, and Stars*. "It's only a primer. Mere child's play. But it's where you must begin. There is much to learn for an apprentice like you, who knows so little."

*The Sun, Moons, and Stars was "a mere primer..."*

Rich sat down cross-legged on the observatory floor and reluctantly dug in. Astronomy confused him and he quickly realized that the book was for experts. It was hard going, and when daybreak's light stirred the far hills, he felt none the wiser.

There was no time for sleepy Rich to snooze. The wocs needed milking, the ne-chick eggs needed gathering, and the breakfast needed cooking. But a young man can go a night without sleep, and Rich did his work without complaint. In fact, he was curious to see how Red Barn would react to Rune's sad news and which villager would ask a question "worthy" of Rune's attention that day.

Red Barn was the first in the long line of villagers, and Rune delivered his verdict immediately, making no effort to soften the blow.

"Your boy is better suited for the plow than the university. He will fail the exam. Such it was, is, and ever shall be. The heavens never lie. *Now go home and do what you must.*"

Red Barn was clearly disappointed, but took the news in stride. "At least I know the truth now," he thought bravely, "and I can act on it."

Rune dismissed sixty-four questions that morning as "a waste of time" before accepting the inquiry of an old woman named Grechet, who was rapidly losing her eyesight.

"My doctor says he can cure me, but the treatment is expensive. Tell me, should I follow his advice, or am I destined to go blind anyway?"

"It's a *worthy* question," Rune pronounced, as he sent the other villagers away. "I will consult with Celestia. That bright, three-mooned planet controls such things.

When you come back tomorrow, I'll have your answer."

Grechet was delighted. After weeks and weeks of asking "unworthy" questions, she'd finally stumbled on a good one. She was thrilled that *her* question would be the topic of Rune's undivided attention that evening— and with a fine new apprentice at his side, too.

After she and the other villagers left, Rune gave Rich his new orders for the day.

"Chop down a tree and split it to make firewood for the winter. There is much to do for an apprentice like you. Now get to work!"

Rich complied, bringing the axe down more times than he could count, until his muscles burned. He'd watched the palace workers create firewood, but he was surprised at how exhausting the labor was.

Meanwhile, Rune put his feet up, delighted that he didn't have to chop the wood himself.

Rich returned to the house that evening completely worn out, but Rune gave him no rest.

"Roast some meat to-night," he commanded. "There is much to do. Get busy."

Rich slaved over the stove

*Rich chopped down a mighty tree...*

and Rune enjoyed another tasty meal. Then, as before, Rune (bespectacled, begowned, and behatted) led Rich up to the observatory.

This time, the crafty man fetched a pair of never-used binoculars from a hook on the wall. They were badly out of alignment (having never been aligned), but Rune claimed to be able to see Celestia through them perfectly.

"The planet is shaped like a sickle," Rune informed Rich. "That's all the information I need to do my work."

Rich frowned. Celestia had phases, just like Urth's two moons, Lunera and Ru, because it was between Urth and its sun. But it was too high in the west to be in its crescent phase. He'd learned all about it the night before in *The Sun, Moons, and Stars*. He thought his studies had been waste of time, but perhaps not!

"May I see for myself?" he asked, suddenly suspicious of Rune.

"All in good time," Rune replied, with a dismissive wave of his hand. "It takes many Ru months to learn how to use my multifarious instruments. For now, you must simply observe what I do, not expect to be part of my expert astrovisioning."

"What fool can't operate a pair of binoculars?" Rich wondered as he watched Rune scribble another fifteen pages of equations, each symbol stranger than the next. "I may not be a whiz at moons-studies, but I've used binoculars often enough."

Just before midnight, Rune heaved a sigh of

satisfaction and circled his final answer: forty-nine.

"The medication won't help Grechet," he announced. "She's fated to go blind."

Rich headed for the stairs, but Rune restrained him.

*Rune circled the number 49 and announced his result...*

"No ducky sack for you," he snapped. "Get back to your studying."

Rich opened his mouth to protest, but he kept his tongue. He was an apprentice, after all, and had no choice, so he dutifully studied *The Sun, Moons, and Stars* until dawn, just as he'd done the night before.

Come morning, he did his chores again, yawning and rubbing his eyes all the while. Then he followed Rune out of the house, where Grechet was standing, first in line, prepared to learn her destiny.

"Don't waste your money," Rune intoned, as she wept. "Such it was, is, and ever shall be. The heavens never lie. *Now go home and do what you must.*"

Grechet disappeared down the hill, following the crooked road that led to town. As she went, many of the villagers reached out to console her. Meanwhile, Rune went through his usual rigmarole, rejecting dozens of questions before accepting one from a pregnant woman named Sailou.

"Is my unborn baby healthy?" Sailou asked. "It's a

bit small in my womb, or so my midwife says."

"It is a *worthy* question," Rune pronounced. "One that requires expert astrovisioning. I shall consult Saros. That ringed planet controls such things."

Oh, thank you, thank you," Sailou cried, clasping her hands. "You're so kind."

Rich spent the rest of the day cleaning the purple house from top to bottom while Rune took it easy. Then he cooked dinner as before and joined Rune in the observatory, where the crooked man faked his way through another wasted evening. But this time, Prince Rich wasn't fooled. Rune's scribblings were clearly gibberish. They looked nothing like the equations in *The Sun, Moons, and Stars.*

*Circling the number 2, Rune was prepared to deliver the terrible news...*

Circling the number two, Rune declared that Sailou's baby would be tiny and scrawny. Then he descended to his bedroom once more, ordering drowsy Rich to stay behind and study up.

The following morning, Rune delivered the cruel news to Sailou.

"Such it was, is, and ever shall be," Rune told the distraught woman. "The heavens never lie. *Now go home and do what you must.*"

Curiously, there were no other villagers waiting for Rune that morning.

Rich asked him why.

"It's market day and the villagers are busy selling and trading their goods. It's my day off, but you'll be busy enough. I have a long shopping list for you."

Rich took the list and the fifteen tidbits Rune gave him to spend, and headed off to the market. Meanwhile, Rune played a crooked game of solitaire, cheating himself out of all his winnings before cheating himself in return to get them back, pleased that he didn't have to go shopping himself.

Rich had never been to a market. The jostling and bargaining confused him. When the clock in the village square struck noon, he bought a hunk of cheese and a small loaf of fresh bread. Then he sat down in the village square for a rest.

As he ate, Red Barn approached him, his wife at his side.

"Our son Nimos is not the bright boy we thought he was," Red Barn remarked.

"It's unhappy news," agreed his wife, "but at least we have a path forward. I sold his textbooks this morning and burned his notes. Tomorrow we'll send him to work in the fields. When he fails the exam in two weeks' time, we'll pay Rune his fee and that will be that. Please thank your master for us."

Rich frowned. He immediately saw the hole in her logic.

"Of *course* Nimos will fail his exams if you don't

*"I burned his notes," she said...*

let him study," he pointed out. "Why not give him a chance?"

"A chance?" Red Barn repeated after him. "Why would we do that? Don't you see? There'd be no point. You can't argue with the heavens." Then he tipped his hat, putting an end to their conversation, and, taking his wife's arm, walked away.

Rich had a keen, rational mind, and was taken aback. Red Barn and his wife were ensuring that Rune's prediction would come true. Frustrated, he finished his lunch and made his way to a stall, where a man was selling apples.

As he negotiated the price for the six apples on Rune's list, Grechet suddenly appeared at his side.

"I refused the medicine," she informed him, with a smile. "Please thank Rune, as he saved me a great deal of money. When I lose my sight, as I'll surely do, I'll pay him his fee and that will be that."

Once again, Rich saw the flaw in her reasoning.

"Naturally, you'll go blind if you don't let the doctor treat you," he exclaimed. "Give the medicine a try. You never know. Rune might be wrong."

"Wrong?" Grechet parroted, picking up an apple and holding it close to her face, where she could see it. "That's impossible. Rune's predictions always come true. You can't fight your fate, young man. The future is written in the stars."

Grechet squeezed Rich's arm in a motherly way and then left him, hobbling down the street rather uncertainly, because she could barely see where she was going.

Rich stood stock still, his sharp mind in overdrive. He'd suddenly seen how Rune was tricking the villagers, and it was a clever method, indeed!

"Rune only accepts a question if the outcome is under the control of the questioner," Rich thought. "Then, when he delivers his prediction, the client, thinking he has no choice, carries it out. 'Go home and do what you must,' the wicked man tells his clients. Oh, he is doing the devil's work."

Determined to expose Rune as the fraud that he was, Rich ignored the rest of his crooked master's shopping list and immediately set off for the purple house.

"I *must* free the villagers from Rune's tyranny," he thought angrily. "But it won't be easy. They're under his clever spell and quite helpless to see it."

A few miles along, Rich ran into Sailou. She was standing beside the road, talking with a neighbor who was also pregnant.

"I won't be drinking our farm's rich milk any longer," she was saying. "I'll give it to you, all four bottles, so your baby will be strong. Mine is destined to be weak, you see, so why waste it?"

In dismay, Rich stopped and intervened.

"Can't you see? Your baby will be weak if you don't feed it," he snapped. "For goodness sake, Sailou, wake up. Rune's a con man. His prediction will come true, but only if you make it so. Drink the milk and prove him wrong. Someone's got to stand up to him!"

Sailou looked at him sorrowfully.

"You can't fight the stars," she said softly. "Everyone knows that. When my unlucky baby comes into the world, it will be weak as a kitten. Then I'll pay Rune his fee, and that will be that."

Rich tried to reason with her, making one good argument after another. He told her about Red Barn. He told her about Grechet. But she refused to listen.

"Remember, you're just an apprentice," the neighbor pitched in, rallying to her friend's defense (for she wanted the milk). "Rune is the skilled astro-futurist (or whatever), not you."

Rich was dismayed, but he didn't push his view any further. It would be impossible to sway the two women.

"It's Rune's day off," he thought, "so there'll be no trip to the observatory tonight. I'll have time to hatch a plan to bring the man to his knees, for it must be done."

Rich chewed on the problem all night long, finally turning to *The Sun, Moons, and Stars* for inspiration. Books often carried secret messages. Starting with chapter one, he picked out the first letter of the sixth word of the first paragraph and linked it to the first letter of the first word of the second paragraph, as he'd been taught to do. Then he repeated the process for the second chapter and so on (the *Sun, Moons, and Stars* had ten chapters in all) and strung the letters together:

## THISBOOKISFOREXPERTS

"Oh!" he cried in frustration, "that's no help whatsoever. I'm so stuck."

The following morning, much to his surprise, Rich heard the merry bugling of the royal army. The king and a large party had made the journey to Rune's village and had set up their colorful tents in the village square.

His father was so eager to meet Rune that he'd

followed closely on Rich's heels, not waiting for him to report back.

Rich was vastly relieved. He would explain everything to his father and let *him* deal with Rune.

But the king refused to listen.

*The king and a large party had set up tents in the village square...*

"I questioned many of the villagers this morning, and they all said the same thing. Rune's predictions always come true. I've made up my mind about the man. I'm taking him back to the palace tomorrow morning, where he'll be more valuable to me than a mountain of gold."

"But father, you don't understand," Rich pleaded. "Rune is as wicked as he is clever. I've seen him in action. He manipulates the villagers shamelessly. If we don't stop him immediately, a boy will be robbed of his education, a woman will go blind, and an unborn child will come to great harm."

"*If* that were true," King Nad replied with a troubled frown, "I'd throw him in jail this minute! I don't tolerate evil men who prey on the gullibility of simple folk for profit! But the people love him. They trust him. And, my dear son, they know him *much* better than *we* do. Why, you've been here only a few days, but they've lived with Rune all their lives."

Prince Rich tried to argue further, but King Nad turned to talk to one of his counselors, bringing the discussion to an abrupt close.

"Father is so afraid of suffering another grievous loss that he's willing to believe Rune, just like the others," Prince Rich thought unhappily. "It's up to me to do something, and quickly. Once Rune is settled in at the palace, it will be impossible to get rid of him."

Prince Rich Satin's mind raced this way and that, searching for a solution. He'd have to *show* his father, and all the villagers, that Rune was a fraud. Words weren't going to convince them. But how could he trick a crooked man who was so skilled at trickery himself?

He pondered the problem all day, considering and rejecting one idea after another. It was hard work, but in the late afternoon, just as he'd decided it was all for naught, inspiration finally struck.

"It's a dangerous plan," he thought nervously. "It could backfire. But I must try. If it works, the people will lose their faith in Rune, and the evil astro-trickster (or whatever) will lose his power over them."

The first step was to talk to his father, so Rich took a seat beside him at dinner, where the king could scarcely ignore him.

"I hate to tell you this," Prince Rich Satin whispered, "but Rune is completely dependent on that purple robe of his. Without it, he can't astro-sense (or whatever). Yet it's frayed along the edges. It's coming apart at the seams. But he refuses to mend it because if he does, it will lose its magic."

King Nad was disturbed by the news. His son had never lied to him before, so he had no reason not to trust his word.

"I don't much like that the man's talents are tied to a robe. Robes don't last forever. I must find out more about this matter, directly from him, so I can make a good decision."

Intent on his purpose, he called Rune to his side before the meal was over.

"You must consult the stars tonight, and find out whether your purple robe will hang together for at least another year. I've heard from a reliable source that you're entirely dependent on it for your work, and it will lose its magic if you mend it."

Rune started to protest, but the king cut him off.

"Go on now. Come back tomorrow."

Rune was greatly confused. Why was the king so worried about his purple robe? He could fashion another without much trouble. He knew how to use a needle and thread. But he did as the king commanded. After all, the request presented no threat. He could easily get around it.

"I'll go back to my purple house and pretend to astrovision all night long," he chuckled. "Then I'll rejoin the king and *do what I must*, mending my robe in secret, once I get to the palace, so it lasts a lifetime."

His mind at ease, Rune went away, snoozing with one eye on the door in case the king sent someone to check on him.

At dawn, he closed up his purple house ("for the last time," he snickered, with satisfaction), walked down the hill, and presented himself to the king once more. He was wearing his purple robe, and he fancied he looked quite fine despite its well-worn condition.

The villagers crowded around as the king greeted Rune.

"And so?" King Nad asked, probing Rune's face for the answer. "What did the heavens say about your robe?"

"Oh, don't worry, your Majesty. Don't worry. My robe will have a long life, a long one, indeed. It's a magical robe, and will last for hundreds of years, in one piece. Such it was, is, and ever shall be. It is written in the stars, and the heavens never lie."

"Are you absolutely sure?"

"Oh, yes, one hundred percent certain. Whatever fears you had in that regard, you can put them to rest."

"That's excellent news!" cried the king, getting to his

feet with a sigh of relief. "I will take you back to the palace, today, and appoint you the royal astro-astrologer."

"**Astrovisionary,** your majesty," Rune corrected him, with a groveling smile and a toadying little bow. "Astrologers and other quacks tell you what *might* happen, but astrovisionaries, like me, tell you what *will*."

Prince Rich, thrilled that Rune had walked directly into the clever trap he'd set for him, suddenly stepped forward.

"You're not the prophet you say," he cried. "You lie. Your astrovisioning is a sham and nothing more. I'll expose you for the quack that you *really* are, so all can see!"

Then, to the astonishment of everyone, he pulled out his sword and sliced Rune's robe off his body (*swish, slash, swish*), leaving the exposed man in his undershorts.

The robe, now in shreds, lay between Rune and the king. As the two men stared at it in disbelief, a wind came up and blew the strips of forlorn fabric away, over the heads of the stunned villagers.

The king was so shocked that he couldn't speak, and a terrible silence followed while he tried to make sense of things. Rich feared that his father might turn on him, failing to see that Rune, himself, had been his own undoing.

"If my father and the people of this village don't understand," he thought determinedly, "so be it. I've done my best. My father gave me a mission and I carried it out. What else could I have done?"

The wind continued to gust, and several of the villagers lost their hats. The king remained silent and shaken, while Rune tried to cover his knobby knees. He was quite vain.

All eyes were on Rune, who looked humbled, indeed. But no one said anything. For Prince Rich Satin, the wait was difficult to bear. His heart pounded with fear, but he stood erect, nobly prepared for whatever came next.

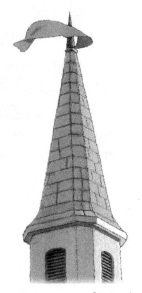

Finally, a maiden—a spritely, intelligent woman not much older than Rich—spoke up, and loudly.

*Fragments of Rune's robe flapped from the church steeple...*

"Maybe Rune can't read the stars after all," she suggested, mirroring the dawning realizations of many of the others. "He certainly got the prediction about his *robe* wrong, didn't he? Very wrong! He said his robe would last for hundreds of years, but it's in hundreds of *pieces* now. Why, look. There's a long strip of it caught on the church steeple!"

Collectively, the villagers redirected their gaze from Rune to the steeple. Then they began murmuring among themselves.

"Nimos!" Red Barn suddenly shouted, his voice rising above the rest. "Maybe Rune's prediction was wrong about him, too.  Maybe Nimos is as smart as he seems and he can pass his entrance exam after all!"

The whispering of the crowd grew louder and angrier, and Prince Rich felt the momentum shift in his favor.

"My *eyesight!*" Grechet cried, grabbing the arm of the man standing next to her. "Oh, please, fetch my doctor. There may yet be time to save it."

On the heels of Gretchet's words came a wail from elsewhere in the crowd. It was Sailou.

"My baby!" she screamed, suddenly catching on. "Someone, fetch me a bottle of rich milk. I've foolishly given mine to a neighbor."

With that, the crowd erupted in turmoil, each villager recounting a time when Rune had given them advice—advice that might have been wrong! Had he been tricking them all along? Would their lives have been better if they hadn't listened to him?

Rune, sensing that he'd been exposed in more ways than one, tried to slip away, but the king's guards stopped him.

"You're not going anywhere," King Nad told him firmly. "Not until we sort this out."

Prince Rich avoided his father's gaze, but gradually, as his father began talking with the villagers individually, hearing their tales of woe, he relaxed. His father was a fair, intelligent ruler. He could see that that villagers were suspicious, now, and it wasn't long before he'd changed his mind, too.

"Lock up that astro-imposter (or whatever)," he ordered his guards. "I can see full well that he's not what he claims to be."

Then, chagrined at his own folly, he took Prince Rich aside to apologize.

"I should have listened to you," he said.

Prince Rich forgave his father instantly and asked him what he planned to do.

"We'll stay one Ru month to help the villagers adjust to life without Rune. They must learn to stand on their own two feet and take responsibility for their decisions, which will be hard for them at first. Then, on the final night, we'll have a feast in your honor. You surely deserve it."

Many of the villagers demanded to see Rune so they could dump their anger on him directly. A few pleaded with King Nad to drag him into the village square and hang him. But the king followed the Rule of Law. Rune Oft would stand trial before the royal court. The villagers would have their revenge, and rightly so, but not quite yet.

The villagers fumed for the next few weeks, reliving the many times that Rune had led them astray. He'd destroyed many dreams—even lives—over the years, and they were livid. But by and by, a few began admitting that they, too, owned some responsibility for the crooked affair.

"I chose fantasy over reality," Red Barn confessed, hanging his head in shame. "What fool would be such a coward?"

"Us, that's who," said Red Barn's wife, taking his hand in fellowship. "We all fell for Rune's lies. It was weak of us, and we suffered greatly for it."

By the time the king's party was set to leave, everyone had come around to the same realization and, united in their gratitude to Prince Rich Satin, flocked to the king's feast.

When the square was full, and the people were ready to eat, King Nad held up a goblet of wine and made a toast.

"Prince Rich Satin," he declared proudly, "has saved you, and this kingdom, from a master schemer. Rune is a wicked astro-fraud (or whatever) and we're lucky to be rid of him. He couldn't foretell the future, nor can anyone, and my son—who has proved himself well and will be your next king—is the hero who showed us that."

# 7

# True Tale at the Equator

*In which a star-crossed prince and an unlucky princess end a war of a thousand years.*

our thousand years ago, at roughly equal distances from the equator, Urth had two mighty civilizations: a queendom in the north, called Glanden, and a kingdom in the south, called Usalariat.

You probably don't know about that distant era. You're from Earth, after all, and don't study Urth history in school. But Urth people know it was a tumultuous period, marked by a war of a thousand years. You see, the Glandenites insisted that waxing moons are lit on the right-hand side, while the Usalariats claimed just the opposite, and the two sides couldn't agree to disagree.

On a planet with two moons, moons-cycles are wickedly complicated, and many children fail their moons-studies course the first time through. But it's

**GLANDEN: WANING**        **GLANDEN: WAXING**
**USALARIAT: WAXING**       **USALARIAT: WANING**

important that they persevere. Moons-cycles control the timing of the harvests and the periodic "syzygy" flooding that comes when Urth's moons and sun align. Thus, moons-tutors have always been in high demand and are paid a princely sum for their services.

In case you need some help with moons, here's a primer: When a moon is *waxing*, it gets bigger with each passing day, shapeshifting from a slender crescent to a glorious full moon in about half a month. Then it switches and begins to *wane*, gradually shrinking from a full moon to a slender crescent, until it disappears over the dawn horizon, only to reappear in the evening sky a day or two later as a slender waxing crescent, ready to start the cycle all over again.

In the time of the Glandenites and Usalariats, science was in its infancy, and people were superstitious. They believed, for example, that "moons-patterns" controlled

*A complete moon-cycle from full moon to new.*

a baby's fate in life. Infants born when both Lunera and Ru were waxing ("double-waxers") were destined to reach their full potential, while those born when both moons were waning ("double-waners") were marked for a dismal future.

Therefore, when the Queen of Glanden became pregnant, and the royal physician, a tall woman named Nan, predicted that her child would be a double-waxer, everyone rejoiced. Her husband (who had no title) was as proud as a man could be.

*Two waxing moons lit on the right...*

"Let's hope it's a girl," the people of Glanden whispered to one another. "In a queendom, it's the girls that matter. And a princess born under two waxing moons (both lit on the *right*, of course) will become a great queen."

Meanwhile, down south in Usalariat, the king's subjects were likewise beside themselves with joy. The king's

*Two waxing moons lit on the left...*

wife (who had no title) was round with child, and the royal physician, a short man named Tap, foretold that the baby would be double-waxer. How lucky!

"Let's pray for a boy," the king's subjects murmured. "In a kingdom, it's the boys we want, and a prince born under two waxing moons (both lit on the *left*, of course) will be a fine king one day."

As fate would have it, all the people (both north and south) were bitterly disappointed. The Queen of Glanden gave birth earlier than expected. Her son, Prince Anthony, was a double-waner. Likewise, the wife of the King of Usalariat surprised her midwife, birthing a princess named Laurette, who was a double-waner, too.

"Our little prince Anthony won't amount to a hill of beans," Queen Glanden's husband prophesized sadly.

*Nan hurried star-crossed Anthony to the*
*royal nursery...*

"It's true," the queen agreed, handing off her new-born dismissively to Nan, who hurried him off to the royal nursery. "It's a tragedy. We must try to have a daughter, who is a double-waxer, and forget about this."

The King of Usalariat was likewise upset and wanted nothing to do with his tiny daughter.

"It would be better if Princess Laurette had never been born," he told his wife. "Let Tap raise her in the highest turret of the castle, out of view. We'll focus our energies on having a son who's a double-waxer. It's the key to keeping the royal line intact and ensuring the well-being of our people."

*Tap disappeared up the stairs with poor, unlucky Laurette...*

Tap reached down and took Laurette in his arms.

"You come with me, little one. I'll care for you," he promised. Then he disappeared up the stairs with her.

As the years passed in the north, Nan dutifully took over Anthony's mothering and came to love him dearly.

"You're a delight to my eyes," she told him. "You have hair the color of fire daisies and blue eyes that remind me of the sky on a bright summer's day. If only your moons-pattern were favorable you'd have everything going for you."

Despite Nan's hopeless outlook, however, she made sure that Anthony was well-educated, recruiting the finest tutors in the land. And because moons don't control a child's fate any more than an ant can move a mountain (though the Glandenites didn't know that), the prince thrived and grew into a handsome, bright young man.

Meanwhile, Tap grew to love Laurette as if the child were his very own. The little girl was high-spirited and smarter than a whip. So, although he knew she'd never become what she might have been had her moons-pattern been a happy one, he hired one brilliant scholar after another to teach her what they could.

"You're a wonder to behold," he often told her. "Your hair is the color of a moons-less night and you have warm brown eyes that remind me of Mother Urth herself. How sad that you're a double-waner, as you surely deserve a better fate than you will get."

Tap was sure that he was right about Laurette's future, but the actual outcome was different. Laurette blossomed, for moons don't control a child's fate any more than a gnat can eat the sun (though the Usalariats didn't know that), and with Tap's excellent care, she reached her full potential just fine.

"How I wish my moons-pattern was different," Laurette often lamented, believing there was something wrong with her. "It's so unfair. I'm nearly grown, but I'll have no chance of living a normal life. I'll never fall in love and have children of my own. I'll be holed up in this castle until I'm an old woman."

In Glanden and Usalariat, Urth children didn't "rename" themselves when they were children, as they do today. Instead, they had to wait until they got married. Therefore, Prince Anthony and Princess Laurette resigned themselves to never being able to make their own decisions. They would be powerless forever.

Even so, the Queen of Glanden didn't give up on her son entirely. She thought about him now and then, and when she did, she felt guilty.

"Anthony is nearly a man now," she pointed out to her husband one day. "Although he'll never amount to much, I'd like to see him married, and renamed. Perhaps some desperate girl—a dumb, ugly one—will take him. It's worth a try, don't you think? I'm going to send out a call to my people and try to snare such a young woman."

Calling all young, unmarried maidens in the queendom! This is your opportunity to marry Prince Anthony and become a princess yourself. Come to the palace at once if you're interested. – Queen of Glanden

Her maidservants carried out her wishes immediately, as she was the ruler of the land. But no girls answered her plea. By then, rumors had circulated that

Prince Anthony was a hunchback with buckteeth and a wicked temperament. Only his tutors and his governess had ever seen him, so the people knew no different.

The King of Usalariat felt similarly guilty and sent out a call on behalf of Laurette. But because she was widely known to be a gangly, half-brained nitwit with a demeanor as sour as a lemon, he got no takers.

Calling all young, unmarried men in the kingdom! This is your opportunity to marry Princess Laurette and become a prince yourself. Come to the palace at once if you're interested. – King of Usalariat

Unfairly, and cruelly, misjudged, Prince Anthony and Princess Laurette might have lived lonely, miserable lives and died too soon, winking out like two waning moons retreating behind the sun. Fortunately, luck shone on them. There was a clever man in Glanden at that time, named Semos, who understood the royal plight and had an inspired idea, one that he hoped would make him quite rich. The queen rewarded her subjects when they served her well, and he wished to be on the receiving end of her generosity.

"I'd like an audience with the queen," he said, when he arrived at the castle's great gate. "Tell her I can solve the problem of Prince Anthony's future."

The queen, now desperate, agreed to the meeting.

"Let him in," she told her gatekeeper. "I'll listen to anyone who has an idea, even a commoner."

A few minutes later, Semos was ushered before her.

Semos curtseyed, as male subjects did in the presence of a queen in a queendom.

"Your Majesty," he said, when she gave him permission to speak, "I believe I have found a young woman who will marry Prince Anthony. And what's more, the marriage will put an end to the Great War between Glanden and Usalariat that has raged for so long."

"What are you saying, man?" asked the queen, intrigued. "How on urth do you propose that I solve both great problems at once?"

Semos cleared his throat. In truth, he was a bit nervous standing before a queen, though he tried to appear otherwise.

"As you know," he continued, "the Usalariats are ignorant. They think that children born under two moons lit on the left are double-waxers. They mistakenly believe such children are destined for greatness."

"Yes, yes, I've heard that," the queen agreed, one eyebrow raised in disdain. "They live in a dark age down there. I learned all about their upside-down thinking from my tutors."

"And that's the point," Semos replied. "I believe you can use their stupidity to your advantage. You see, the King of Usalariat has a daughter who's a double-waxer, but *he* believes she's a double-waner. He believes she has no potential. Laurette is her name, and (as we know) she must be quite wonderful given her favorable moons-pattern. But her father locks her up in a high turret and thinks she's not worth his time."

The queen pondered this.

"The King of Usalariat has a daughter who was born under two moons lit on the right-hand side," she thought, "the best moons-pattern of all. Yet *he* thinks she was born under the *worst* moons-pattern. How interesting!"

The queen was no fool, and she sensed immediately that Semos had stumbled onto something important. Perhaps something very important, indeed.

For his part, Semos could see that he had the queen's attention, so he continued unabated:

"The King of Usalariat will jump at the chance to marry Laurette to our Prince Anthony. He'll think Anthony is a prize catch for her!"

The queen understood Semos' plan perfectly, and having a taste for irony, began to laugh. In fact, she laughed and laughed and laughed until tears were coursing down her cheeks and she was scarcely able to breathe.

Semos laughed, too, and then continued, craftily:

"It's difficult to end a protracted war that has drained the royal coffers. Any queen who can do that is a great leader. If you follow my counsel, you will be remembered for generations as the ruler who managed to do it."

He failed to add that he was looking forward to a

reward for his cleverness. *That*, he figured, would follow in due course.

The queen got stars in her eyes then. *Stars of ambition.* The idea that Glandenites would forever celebrate her as the greatest queen of all time captured her imagination. Quickly, she ordered the royal scribe to draft a letter to the King of Usalariat, outlining Semos' proposition as if it were her own (which, by then, she was convinced it was).

*The paddle-saddler delivered the
queen's message post-haste...*

The fastest "paddle-saddler" in the queendom was dispatched to deliver the message post-haste, and because she was a very fast paddler indeed, she was standing before the King of Usalariat just two Lunera months later, dripping and exhausted, with the queen's important offer in her hand. She'd transported the scroll in a waterproof "pod" around her neck, and now she opened the pod and removed the scroll for all to see.

"What is this?" boomed the king, staring at the foreign woman with the fancy scroll. "A *female* paddle-saddler?

I've never heard of such a thing."

The paddle-saddler bowed with a flourish.

The king grew even more displeased. Women didn't *bow* in his kingdom. They curtseyed. But he gave her the benefit of the doubt when he learned that she was from Glanden. After all, Glandenites were ignorant, superstitious folk. It was no wonder she didn't know how to behave properly in front of a king.

"Your Majesty," the paddle-saddler explained, "it's typical in my country for women to do this kind of work. In the Queendom of Glanden, women do almost everything."

"Yes, yes. But why have you come to Usalariat?" he thundered. "Our countries are at war."

"To deliver a proposal, straight from Her Majesty's hand," the paddle-saddler replied, in a matter-of-fact tone that belied her fear at being the only Glandenite in the crowd. "I think you'll find it interesting."

The king's eyebrows shot up. No queen of Glanden had communicated directly with a king of Usalariat for hundreds of years.

"What crazy claim is this?" he cried. "It's impossible. Stop telling lies, or I'll cut off your head."

The paddle-saddler bowed once more, and then proceeded to clarify.

"My queen wishes to end the Great War by uniting our countries through marriage. Her son, Prince Anthony—who was born under two moons lit on the *left* by the way—is the same age as your daughter, Princess Laurette. It's all written down in this scroll. My royal queen awaits your royal answer."

The king frowned and consulted briefly with his manservant, who always stood at his side. Then he took the proposition from the paddle-saddler (who was happy to be shed of the responsibility) and read the proposal.

The king was not a stupid man (no matter what the people of Glanden thought of him), and he recognized immediately that the queen's offer was to *his* benefit, not hers.

"The Queen of Glanden thinks Laurette is a fortunate girl and that her own son is a dud, when it's actually the other way around. She thinks she's getting a good bargain with her proposition, when *I'm* the one who's getting the prime deal. What a tidy way to snag a wonderful husband for Laurette, while earning the reputation as the clever, peaceful king who ended the Great War!"

The king could not keep his composure. The situation struck him as deliciously absurd, and he began to laugh. In fact, he laughed and laughed and laughed, until tears were coursing down his cheeks and he was scarcely able to breathe.

Meanwhile, the paddle-saddler waited patiently. She valued her head and hoped that the king would be kind enough to let her keep it.

When the king had recovered from his mirth, he announced his decision.

"It's a fine offer, and I accept it heartily!" he cried. "Let the scribes write up my answer and send the paddle-saddler back home, to deliver my message to the Queen of Glanden."

He swelled with pleasure when the room erupted with applause. A few days later, he'd forgotten the details and was sure that the idea for uniting the two countries was his (and so it went down in history, at least in Usalariat).

The paddle-saddlers of Glanden (all female) and their counterparts in Usalariat (all male) were busy for the next many Lunera months, shuttling messages back and forth between the king and queen. There was a great deal of negotiation (ending a war is no easy task), but both sides were motivated, believing they were getting the best of the other. In the end, they signed a tentative treaty and agreed that Anthony and Laurette would meet on Sogapalaga Island, which lay at the equator, neither north nor south. It was neutral territory and a pleasant spot where the two young people could live, side-by-side, for half a year (the traditional courting period) to see if they could grow to love one another. If they did, the Queen of Glanden and the King of Usalariat agreed to end the war immediately after the wedding.

From that day forward, the Queen of Glanden treated her son with great respect. Meantime down south, in Usalariat, the king ordered four handmaidens to pamper

*Sogapalaga Island was neutral territory*
*neither north nor south...*

Laurette and cater to her every whim.

Both sides built great ships, painting them in vibrant colors befitting a royal engagement, and, on the agreed upon date, sailed them into Sogapalaga Bay under the watchful gaze of curious natives, who disappeared when the foreigners came ashore.

There was a great deal of confusion at first. The women of Glanden, who were accustomed to being in charge, tried to boss the men of Usalariat about, while the men of Usalariat, who ruled the roost at home, countered by doing the same. In the end, however, they managed to work around their differences. Each side feared that any disturbance might compromise the first promise of peace they'd had in centuries, and everyone longed for the Great War to end.

After the king and queen agreed on a draft treaty, the king bowed (he didn't curtsey) and the queen bowed (she didn't curtsey) and the deed was done. Everyone returned to their ships and sailed home (north or south depending on their origins), except Anthony and Laurette, who were left with instructions to fall in love if they possibly could, as the treaty to end the war would only be finalized if they did.

Anthony was nervous. He'd heard terrible things about Laurette from the Usalariats. He didn't know if he could marry a gangly, half-brained nitwit with a demeanor as sour as a lemon.

Likewise, Princess Laurette was anxious, too. The Glandenites had painted a similar, troubling portrait of Prince Anthony. Who could marry a hunchback with buckteeth and a wicked temperament?

These lies about them were ridiculous, and the two young people realized it the moment they set eyes on one another.

They were both shy and lacked self-esteem, having lived in shame behind closed doors most of their lives, so they took their courtship slowly. They didn't rush across the room and hug one another in relief. Instead, they kept their distance and agreed to take a walk together under the evening sky to moons-gaze and familiarize themselves with Sogapalaga Island and each other. It was impossible to see the sky from the lush, tropical forest, so they headed for the highest hill on the island, where they'd have a good view.

At first, neither spoke, but finally Laurette broke the silence.

"My birth was unlucky," she began, determined to tell Anthony the bitter truth up front, rather than hide it from him. "I was born under two moons lit on the *right*, you see. I'm a double-waner, no proper match for a double-waxer like you. I'm sorry my father put you in such a position."

Anthony was astonished.

"I don't understand," he replied. "*I'm* the double-waner, not you. I was born under two moons lit on the *left*, you see."

"Then you're a double-waxer, not a double-waner," Laurette countered.

"No. *You're* the double-waxer," he argued, with equal conviction.

It was an awkward moment. They were talking at cross-purposes. Moons-patterns were difficult enough to understand without all the "double-waxer," "double-waner" terminology their tutors had taught them.

It took them a few moments to get their bearings, but Laurette suddenly remembered something that Tap hold told her, long ago, when she was a girl.

"Oh, Anthony, I think I understand," she said gently. "Your people believe that waxing moons are lit on the *right*, don't they? It's a superstition. I've studied astronomy since I was a toddler. Waxing moons are lit on the *left*. This truth of nature can't be denied, but it's good news for you. It means you're a double-waxer after all, and no wonder, as you're so handsome."

"Not so," Anthony argued. "My tutors took me moons-gazing all the time. I passed the entrance exam for the Moons Academy, which is no easy task. Waxing moons are lit on the *right*."

They both fell silent, unsure how to break the stalemate.

"We've known each other less than an hour, and we're already arguing," thought Laurette. "That can't be a good sign."

"Ru should be up now," Anthony finally pointed out, his logical mind winning out over his befuddled one. "It's in its first quarter phase, so it's waxing. Can we agree to that at least?"

"Yes," Laurette replied. "When we left Usalariat a week ago, Ru was new. So it must be at first quarter now. I'm glad we've found some common ground at last."

Anthony was relieved, too.

"So," he continued in rational fashion, "if it's lit on the right then *my* people are correct, and if it's lit on the left *yours* are."

Laurette was certain that Ru would be lit on the left (she would have staked her life on it), so as they climbed out of the forest and up a grassy hill, she strode in confidence.

Anthony, equally sure that Ru would be lit on the right (he would have staked his life on it), kept up with her, just as eager to make his point.

Only one of them could be correct, and it turned

*Ru was lit on the right!*

out to be Anthony. Ru was high in the dusky sky when it came into view, and there was no doubt! It was lit on the *right!*

A chill ran straight through Laurette, and her mouth fell open.

"What?" she cried. "This can't be happening. A first quarter moon lit on the *right?* How can that be?"

Prince Anthony tried to put his arms around her as she broke down and sobbed, moved by fright more than sorrow.

"I can see it's a terrible shock," he said kindly. "You're just confused. A bit backward in your thinking. When you come up for air, everything will make sense again."

Laurette rebuffed him.

"Stop talking to me like I'm a child. Something is terribly wrong here, and it's nothing to do with me."

Anthony tried a few more times to smooth her ruffled feathers, but it was no use. She was inconsolable, and there was nothing to do but turn in for the night and get some rest.

Nights are warm in the tropics, and Anthony decided to sleep under the sky. But Laurette chose to hide beneath a tree, where the orange glare of Ru could not reach her.

Over the next week, they returned to the high hill and Ru repeated its performance, waxing to a full moon over the ensuing evenings, always lit on the *right*. And when Lunera appeared on the western horizon, a slender waxing crescent, it was lit on the right as well. The Glandenites were correct, and Laurette had to admit defeat, her mind a jumble.

On the eighth evening, she'd had enough and refused to go moons-gazing again. Anthony, not wanting to aggravate her, agreed to refrain from it too. He felt vaguely guilty for having the upper hand and was happy to forget about moons for a while. Thus, many months passed when they stayed in the forest, avoiding the moons altogether. Instead, they redirected their curiosities towards each other, enjoying their newfound friendship a little more each passing day until they loved each other and wanted nothing more than to spend the rest of their lives together.

"The paddle-saddlers are due back tomorrow," Laurette said one morning, six months after they'd arrived on the island. "It's time to share our happy news with the world!"

Anthony smiled, took her hands in his, and twirled her around, off her feet.

"Yes. They'll be thrilled that the Great War is coming to an end, but they'll not be as contented as you and I!"

Laurette agreed wholeheartedly, and she felt the last vestiges of distance from Anthony fall away.

"Let's go moons-gazing tonight," she suggested, hardly believing the words as they fell from her mouth.

"Yes, let's," Anthony cried. "I want us to do *every-thing* together from now on, my love. Let's not let the moons come between us."

As it happened, Ru was at first quarter again, so as they climbed the grassy hill, they knew exactly what to expect: it would be lit on the *right*.

But when they crested the final ridge, hand in hand, the Universe surprised them.

"What's this?" Laurette thought in awe, letting go of Anthony's hand and running ahead to reach the summit.

Were her eyes deceiving her?

*No. Ru was lit on the <u>left</u>, just as waxing moons were supposed to be!*

"Anthony!" she cried, turning around excitedly. "Look at Ru. It's lit on the *left!*"

*Ru was lit on the left!*

Anthony, as confused as she was, was right behind her.

"This can't be," he cried. "It's impossible." He felt like someone had snatched Urth from beneath his feet, and he almost toppled over.

Breathless, Anthony and Laurette stared at one another

in the eerie orange Ru-light and then cried in unison:

"But we can't *both* be correct!"

A few moments passed, and Laurette became thoughtful.

"Perhaps the natives of this island can clear up our confusion. They live here and doubtless know things our peoples don't."

Anthony, still shaken, agreed it was a good plan. It was obvious that something strange was happening at the equator, and he was as eager as Laurette to solve the mystery.

Up until then, they'd ignored the natives. Their parents had painted them as dangerous savages. But curiosity was a strong driver, and Anthony and Laurette were beginning to question everything they'd been told by their parents, anyway, so they took the risk.

When they entered the village and stated their need for advice, a friendly woman led them to the hut of an ancient wizard, who was wiser, it turned out, than the wisest Usalariat and smarter than the smartest Glandenite. Like all Urth people, he had lavender skin, but his skin was moderate in color, neither the pale amethyst of Prince Anthony's nor the rich indigo of Laurette's.

"For a thousand years, your peoples have fought over this silly matter," the wizard told them. "Here's the simple truth. In the *southern* latitudes, waxing moons are lit on the left-hand side and waning moons on the right-hand side. But in the *northern* latitudes, just the opposite is true. It's a matter of whether you live north or south of the equator, you see."

Anthony and Laurette stared at him, dumbfounded, but also delighted.

"So we *are* both correct," Laurette cried, grabbing Anthony's hand and squeezing it hard.

Anthony hugged her before turning back to the wizard.

"But what about here, on Sogapalaga Island?" he asked eagerly, sensing they were close to a fuller understanding. "When we arrived here, waxing moons were lit on the right, but now they're lit on the left. It's so confusing."

"Ah, well *that*, my dear boy, is because Sogapalaga Island sits on the equator, neither north nor south. Depending on the time of year, anything goes."

Then he picked up a stick and drew a diagram in the sand that explained everything.

He used terms like *celestial equator, ecliptic, and tilted axis* to make his point, but with their knowledge of astronomy, Anthony and Laurette were able to follow along, marveling that their peoples hadn't realized this truth before.

"They never thought to look past their own latitudes!" Laurette exclaimed, shaking her head. "How close-minded is that?"

Anthony had one more question.

"Who's in charge here, the men or the women? The women have the power in Glanden, but in Usalariat it's quite the opposite."

"We share the load," the wizard replied, shrugging his shoulders. "We Sogapalagans don't pay much heed to the sex of a person. It's what an individual can offer to the community that matters. Male or female, it makes no difference."

The paddle-saddlers arrived the next day, and excitedly left the island a few hours later, one paddling north to Glanden (female) and the other south to Usalariat (male), to spread the best news of their lifetimes.

Semos was happy and expectant; he was sure the queen would grant him a large parcel of land for his wise counsel. But, having decided that the idea for ending the war was hers, she shooed him off, directing the royal accountant to give him a few golden "tidbits" for his effort, barely enough to pay his rent for one Lunera month.

Two Ru months later, the happy couple were wed on the shores of Sogapalaga Island, in a grand ceremony attended by all, including the natives.

"Finally, we can rename ourselves," Anthony beamed, his eyes locked with Laurette's, filled with love.

The Queen of Glanden, right on cue, stepped forward.

The Renaming Ceremony was an ancient one and she knew her role well.

"Prince Anthony!" she boomed, holding her royal sword above his head (as was the custom in Glanden). "What rename do you choose, my son, and what is your Renaming Wish?"

Anthony turned his gaze to his mother and proclaimed, "I choose the rename Yonthan. Yonthan Trees are native to this island, and because my Renaming Wish is to live here with my new bride from now on, the name is a good one."

The queen's eyes widened in surprise. In Glanden, married men went to live with the families of their wives, not to remote islands!

The King of Usalariat was up next, to play his part.

"And *you*, Princess Laurette," he thundered, lowering his sword to touch her toes (as was the custom in Usalariat). "What rename do *you* choose, my daughter, and what is your Renaming Wish?"

"I choose the rename True Tale," she declared without hesitation, "because I know the *true tale* behind the pointless war that's raged between our peoples. And my Renaming Wish is to live here, on Sogapalaga Island, where everyone gets along."

It was the king's turn to be surprised. In Usalariat, married women went to live with the families of their husbands, not to remote islands! But what he found even more troubling was his daughter's attitude.

"Pointless?" he asked. "That is a claim, indeed. Whatever do you mean, True Tale?"

True Tale scanned the crowd for the wizard. She'd alerted him beforehand that she planned to call on him after the Renaming Ceremony, and he was ready.

"Come forward, wise man," she prompted him. "You explained the truth to me and Yonthan. Now it's time for everyone to hear it."

The wizard emerged from the crowd to join True Tale and Yonthan, curtseying to the queen and bowing to the king. He was the only one who knew how to behave in a way that pleased them both, and his fine manners put the monarchs in the mood to listen to him.

The wizard then proceeded, slowly and logically, to lay out his argument, wielding his stick to great effect.

When he was done, a heavy silence fell on the crowd, punctuated only by a loud burp from Semos.

The people of Glanden, dumbfounded, looked to their queen, while the people of Usalariat, astonished, looked to their king. They wanted their rulers to refute the wizard's claims. But the queen and king, avoiding each other's eyes, didn't say a word. Neither was brainless (regardless of what they'd once thought of each other). They knew the wizard was right, and there was no point putting up a fight.

Instead, the king declared that the Great War had

been pointless and that he regretted his foolishness. Then the queen followed suit, accepting her role in the matter, as good rulers do. After that, she linked arms with the king, and they retreated to the great tent behind them, leaving their subjects to figure out what to do next.

"That's settled then," a Glandenite blurted out. "It was a silly war, but now that it's over, let's celebrate!"

Given the great cost of the war to both sides, it was an outlandish thing for her to say. She, herself, had lost a sister in a battle, and a good friend, too. But the crowd seemed to accept it. The cloud of ignorance settled over them almost as quickly as it had dissipated, and each person was as eager for a party as the next.

"Yes!" shouted an Usalariat. "Let's toast the new couple and their Renaming Wishes and the beginning of their life together. It's the tradition of both the Glandenites and the Usalariats, and, now that we're united, we can whoop it up together."

Semos piped up, "It was my idea..." but his voice was lost in the commotion. Someone set off fireworks, and, within moments, everyone was dancing. Soon, the whole island was ringing with sound.

Alone together inside the tent, the Queen of Glanden looked at her throne and the King of Usalariat looked at his. It didn't seem right, to either of them, to take their royal seats as if nothing had happened. It was an unexpected end to the Great War, and they both felt extremely foolish.

HIS                    HERS

*The king had his throne; the queen had hers.*

"My Yonthan is a handsome, intelligent boy, isn't he?" the queen mumbled. "Funny I didn't see that all along."

"And my True Tale is a fine young lady. You and I have been blind," said the king.

"Indeed," she agreed sadly. "We missed getting to know our children when they were young and now they'll be living here, on this far-flung island, distant from us both."

The husband of the Queen of Glanden (who was weeping), came to fetch the queen and they boarded the ship that would ferry them north. Soon after, the wife of the King of Usalariat (who was also weeping) led him back to the ship that would take them south.

But Yonthan and True Tale stayed where they were, on Sogapalaga Island, where they danced together on the beach every night, laughing at how a queendom and a kingdom could be at war for a thousand years, over something as simple as perspective.

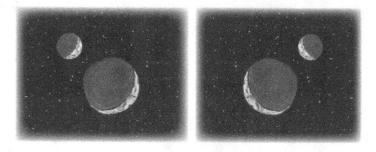

The End

# Glossary and Pronunciation Guide

*(in alphabetical order)*

**Ducky sack:** Soft and comfortable bedding stuffed with luxurious wool or downy feathers.

**G'do ("guh-<u>doo</u>"):** A domesticated animal, much like a dog, famous for its loyalty and keen sense of smell. Plural: g-doos ("guh-dooz").

**Gip:** A domesticated animal raised and traded for its rich, fatty bacon. Plural: Gips. Juvenile: Gipitty.

**Great Melt:** An ecological catastrophe that flooded Urth's vast continents. The polar ice caps melted in a matter of decades, raising sea levels so high that only the tips of mountains and the plains of high mesas remained above the waves.

**Head grass:** A highly nutritious grain.

**Leci ("lek-ee")**: Small white parasites that live in hair and suck on scalp blood. Children are especially vulnerable to infection. Leci is both singular and plural.

**Lunera ("Loo-nair-uh")**: The closer and brighter of Urth's two moons. Lunera appears about twice the diameter of Earth's moon when seen from the planet's surface. Lunera months include (among others) Nuje, Jylu, Ugusta, Tespember, Tocober, Venomber, and Cedember.

**Macel ("mack-ell")**: A beast of burden common to the high mountains of Urt. Plural: Macels. (See Urt, below.)

**Moons-cycle:** The waxing and waning of moons over time.

**Moons-less night:** A night when neither of Urth's two moons is above the horizon. Moons-less nights are wonderful for stars-gazing.

**Moons-lings:** People who live on moons.

**Moons-pattern:** The combined phases of Urth's two moons at any given time. For example, Ru could be a waning crescent while Lunera is at third quarter.

**Moons-studies:** The academic discipline devoted to the study of moons.

**Ne-chick:** Female domestic foul that lays nutritious eggs. Plural: Ne-chicks. Juvenile: Ne-chicklet.

**Nerva ("nerve-uh"):** An intelligent black bird with red eyes. Plural: Nervas.

**Paddle-saddler:** A messenger who delivers mail and other documents by paddling. (See Paddling, below.)

**Paddling:** Swimming.

**Palaca ("pal-uh-kuh"):** A domesticated animal valued for its remarkable wool. Palaca is both singular and plural.

**Picnic grof:** An amphibian that breeds in muddy water and secretes a toxin through its skin. Plural: Picnic grofs. Juvenile: picnic grofling.

**P-sider ("puh-sigh-der"):** A gregarious invertebrate that spins valuable silk. Plural: P-siders. Juvenile: p-siderling.

**Rename:** A new name that a child gives himself when he reaches a certain age. Renaming is an important rite of passage for Urth children (or young adults, depending on the era). Once they rename themselves, they have more control over their fates.

**Renaming Ceremony:** An event, often public, in which children choose their renames. In some cultures, the ceremony is a formal affair; in others, it's quite informal and might be done "on the fly."

**Renaming Rules:** Rules that govern the renaming process. For example, when choosing a rename, a child is limited to the letters in his birth name. Lamar could rename himself Ramal or Laram, for example, but not Johnny or Dwayne. Renames can also be split into more than one word. A girl named Christine could rename herself Nice Shirt. (A fine choice!)

**Renaming Wish:** A wish made by a newly renamed child. A Renaming Wish (unless ridiculous) must be granted. Some children ask for something trivial (like having pancakes for dinner), but clever children use their opportunity more wisely.

**Rewn:** A colorful songbird. Plural: Rewns.

**Ru ("Roo"):** The dimmer and more distant of Urth's two moons. It is orange, and its diameter is about the same as Earth's moon when viewed from the planet's surface.

**Sehor ("See-hoar"):** A domesticated mammal used for pulling carts and riding long distances. Plural: Serhors.

**Serroot ("Suh-root"):** Male domestic foul that fertilizes female ne-chick eggs (to make ne-chicklets) and cries "cock-a-doodle-do." Plural: Serroots.

**Tac:** A domesticated house pet fond of eating. Plural: Tacs.

**Tar:** A small mammal that likes to hang around human dwellings and steal grain and other goodies. Plural: Tars.

**Tidbit:** Gold coin used as currency.

**Urt ("Yert"):** A vast continent that existed before the Great Melt. (See Great Melt, above.)

**Urth ("Yearth"):** A two-mooned planet located 64,000 light years from Earth, on the far side of the Milky Way Galaxy. In the old days (when the events in this book took place), Urth was similar to Earth, with wide oceans, polar ice caps, and vast continents boasting snowy mountains, fertile river valleys, and sandy deserts. In recent times, the Great Melt changed the surface landscape dramatically. Today, Urth is a planet of islands. (See Great Melt, above.)

**Urth people:** Human-like inhabitants of Urth. In the distant past, their ancestors lived exclusively on coastlines and depended on the sea for their survival. As a result, they evolved many marine adaptations: webbed feet (to aid in paddling), a layer of blubber around their mid-sections (to keep them warm and buoyant in water), long, wooly hair (to give children something to hang onto while paddling with their parents), and the ability to hold their breath underwater for half an hour or more. Urth people also have lavender skin, ranging from pale amethyst to deep, rich indigo. (See Urth, above. See Paddling, above.)

**Woc:** Domestic mammal raised for meat and milk. Plural: Wocs. Juvenile: Wocitty.

**Wocboy:** A ranch worker who herds wocs, usually while riding a sehor. (See Sehor, above.)

# About the Author

Ruthy Ballard is a children's book author, artist, and scientist who lives in Sacramento, California. By day, she's "Dr. Ruth Ballard," a professor and forensic DNA expert. By night, she romps in an imaginative playground of colors and words.

Ruthy is the author of *Frankie and the Gift of Fantasy* and *Tales by Moons-Light: Stories from Before the Great Melt*. She is currently working on the third book in her Tales by Moons-light series: *Elvia and the Gift of Passion*.

Her entertaining stories lure middle grade readers into science, but her creative ventures don't stop there. She's also a folk artist whose colorful "cartoons" delight and inspire both children and adults.

Ruthy is married to a musician and is the mother of two sons, three cats, and a Samoyed dog named Mush, all of whom appear in her work, in various guises, from time to time.

Like this book and want more from this author? Visit *www.WhipSmartBooks.com*

and join the Insider's Club. You'll get a free preview of the next book in the series, *Elvia and the Gift of Passion*, enticing book extras, giveaway offers, fun activities and contests, links to upcoming events, and so much more!

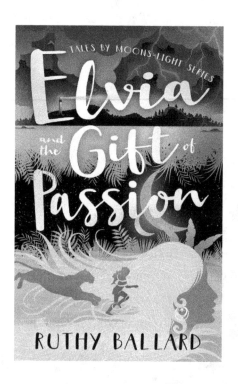